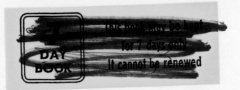

We, the Wilderness

We, the Wilderness

Thomas York

McGraw-Hill Ryerson Limited

Toronto Montreal New York London Sydney Johannesburg
Mexico Panama Düsseldorf Singapore Sao Paulo
Kuala Lumpur New Delhi

We, the Wilderness

Any similarity to any living person is purely coincidental.

ISBN 0-07-077628-8

1 2 3 4 5 6 7 8 9 10   D73 10 9 8 7 6 5 4 3

Printed and bound in Canada

To the wife of my youth and the Indians of Bella Bella

Contents

Principal Families

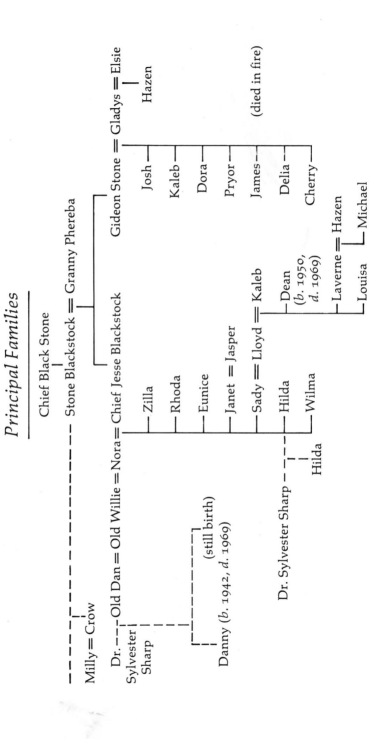

PROLOGUE

Kaleb
Janet
Letty
Lydia

Kaleb

Ground-swell swaying, between sets, or maybe your net's out; slack water so you're dozing between tides. Not many boats and those that are out are way out, trolling or just idling waiting for that run of pinks the Fisheries Department promised: five million pinks that never were (and if they were the seiners would get them) except in the stone traps and blockheads of the old ones and fisheries officials. But it's Tuesday and tomorrow's the weekend, so you're putting in your fifteen two-day weeks like all the rest so the government can call your welfare "unemployment insurance." Money's money, only the government calls it by different names. So you're sitting waiting for a legendary fish, or school of fish, drawing unemployment against the day, not when there are no more fish, but when there are no more myths of fishes. The old ones. Giants in the sea then; this year's pinks so small they pass right through the webbing. Well, I never said they weren't there, I just couldn't catch them. With my radar, sounding gear, power winch and rigging they just passed me by, not rocking the boat. Giant fish (or giant liars?) that flip their tail and the tide shifts, whose passage underneath makes the ground-swell. Peaceful though, getting paid to watch for monsters and knowing you're insured against their surfacing again, if ever they did surface, save in old men's dreams and in the monthly checks we're issued to keep quiet.

I doze and dream of Sady, now a dream, once like everything worth dreaming flesh and blood. Or was she? How much in fifteen years does one remake the one he dreams of, one who actually bore children and got drunk and died, discolored, from gorging on stink-eggs? Such details do not cling to dreams any more than flesh clings to the bone or bone to spirit or whatever is released and surfaces, sometimes, like a lost seascape or a familiar odor. Since everything we loved then is lost now, we can only dream it. Everything.

I dream of Sady: hard flat belly, heavy hips and thighs— like those cedar trees with spreading stumps and narrowing brown trunks. That's the way it is with all our women, they grow earthward. With each child they seem to settle and their breasts sag till by thirty they remind you of the earth. Earth-colored, too, except those lovely long nipples like ripe salmon-berries. A woman's lucky, Sady always said, to die young. Not so young her children are left squalling, but by time they reach school age. . . . She's probably right, she usually was. Anyway, Sady is out gathering seaweed, barefoot because the tidal rocks are slippery and with only a tow-sack slung around her hips to wipe her knife on. A gentle ground-swell rocks the skiff where Dean (he must be four or five) is sitting playing with the oar-locks and dabbling his fingers in the water. Every now and then he calls his mother, holding up some dripping black seaweed; she looks up, stooping, or straightens up and wipes the knife clean on her hips and stretches her long body—seeming to embrace and threaten with the knife the ocean and the world beyond the ocean. Little Louisa watches from the boat; she is afraid of the long knife and holds my hand. And suddenly I hear her name, distinct, not distant: like blood crying out, still crying after fifteen years of dreaming it to sleep. I see her drunk and blood-red, hear her sister, bending over her—

"*Sady D., Sady D., this is Janet Lee*"—as automatically my hand gropes for the radio-phones.

The sudden taste, smell, sickly-sweet and acrid says: It

wasn't the stink-eggs, it wasn't poison she died of; though they pumped her stomach so the nurses wouldn't know, and that was what the doctor told the village. But it wasn't the stink-eggs, it was the blood. I had forgotten. Thinking, so it's come to this after fifteen years of lying. After fifteen years of lying to believe the lie myself. How could I forget a thing like that?

"*Sady D., Sady D., this is Janet Lee.*"

"Go ahead, *Janet Lee.*" I can see the *Janet Lee* with her poles down like arms spread, trolling just inside the banks. Jasper at the wheel I can imagine: five foot three and flanked by nude fold-outs milky white (as close as he will ever get, poor henpecked bastard)—the diminutive male in the cockpit of pleasure. His wife and mine were sisters, that was all.

"I see you got your net out."

"Yeh, just killin' time, scratchin'. How you doin'?"

"Same. Listen, Kaleb. . . ."

Static. Some urgent-voiced Swede sweeps through our band. Another answers, shrill and complaining, then fades away. Swedes suicide so easy.

". . . so I said maybe he's not monitoring, I'll try to pick him up," Jasper is saying. "You there yet?"

"Yeh, I didn't catch you though. We were cut off."

"I said you better take in. Heard Bull Harbor radio the plane, the air-sea boys. *Kilbella IV.* I think it's Dean. Over."

"Yeh, I'll pull in, Jasper. Thanks."

Silence.

"Hope everything's okay at home, Kale. Janet's there if you need her."

"Yeh. Thanks, Jasper."

I never even picked, just wound her in and headed off. If there had been a corpse caught in the net—Jake Trout caught a Swede once—I would have wrapped him with the jelly-fish and seaweed on the drum. I was that scared.

Janet

It can't be, I told myself, it can't be true, not Dean! When it was Danny with his head blown off, I thought, he had it coming. He threatened and threatened and finally he had to do it. But not Dean! Not Sady's Dean! I just couldn't believe it till the air-sea rescue came and we were all down waiting on the dock, it wasn't easy, those Pentecostals gathered like they smelled a second death and Letty, though she's harmless really, scanning with her long fingers the Bible. So on edge I snatched it from her hands.

"It's not a death," I said. "He's been on the fish-boats and probably got his arm caught in a winch." I turned her Bible right-side up and gave it back. "They're just bringing him in to the hospital, it's not a death," I said.

The plane came then, and curious as the Pentecostals were, they moved aside, the stretcher-bearers sliding him out feet first like a breech-birth wrapped already and, naturally, I told myself, a little bloody; a little blood is natural beneath the sheets. Only his feet and head were showing and as he slid toward me I counted toes but before I'd found his hands he was alongside pale and seeping from the middle and his hand found mine and pressed it but the pressure didn't last. I searched the blood-caked stubble where I guess he'd wiped the sweat off and his little boy's grimace was still there as if to say, "See, aren't you proud of me?" and, "Help me!" at the same time, but the look he gave was weak and didn't last. I tried to give a reassuring

look as they hurried him on up the boardwalk to the village
hospital, while seeping from his stomach down the sheet and
through the blanket, spatters of his life-blood fell.

It started raining then and someone, while we walked behind him dripping, said it was a blessing all the blood would
wash away. That started Letty and the Pentecostals singing
Washed in the Blood, yodelling really:

> *Waash'd in the blu-ud,*
> *Waash'd in the blu-ud,*
> *Oh I'm washed in the prechus blud of*
> *Juh-ee-zus!*

They were still singing, wet and crowded in the hospital lobby,
when that other preacher came and lost his glasses and went
scuttling around on hands and knees groping and crying out
"Excuse me!" until Margaret Jenks, I think it was, stepped on
them. The doctor called me in then.

"Janet," he said in that quiet shrinking voice, and before he
spoke the words I heard the tone. "You're his nearest kin until
Kaleb gets here. If you want to call them in," he nodded towards
the lobby with a little bird-like bob, "it's entirely up to you, of
course. Only if you want to. . . ." His voice trailed off and I
thought that he might skitter like a mouse into the woodwork,
but I asked him.

"How bad is he?" I asked. I had to know.

"Liver and kidneys traumatized, internal haemorrhaging,
one lung entirely filled, the other punctured," he sighed deeply,
"we don't have the equipment here, no, not at all." He studied
his watch then, looking down. At last he said, "He might last
out the night. I'm sorry, Janet. Excuse me, I must. . . ." He disappeared into a room where I heard water running.

So that's the way it is, I thought, and this is what it comes

We, the Wilderness

to: Sady, you owe me one more. Since I didn't want to walk in and since Sady had long ago run out, I went back to the lobby. They were waiting. I opened the locked doors to the smell of wet and crowded raincoats and before I could tell them, Letty blurted "Prechus Jesus."

Letty

Ever since I was dreamin' of war that's when I started the prayer. Prayin' for us never to have war 'cause we're one family in the world and we're just s'posed to travel 'round visitin' each other. And I really heard jet planes, but when I went out to look up at the sky there was nothin', just a dream. That's when I was makin' that big silver ball, nineteen pounds, from the gum wrappers. But it burned with my ol' house. Heard one of the men here found it and uses it for trollin'.

Yes, I do love sailors and that hymn about their children. Thou shalt not chase the sailors away, Jesus said that. He told me when their boat was tied up down the dock, and we're s'posed to love each other the whole wide world 'round. But I'm no drunker. That's what I told my ol' drunker-sister and her husband when they lived with me before and tried to force me. "I'd rather wait for Jesus' wine," I said, "Jesus' wine is better than ol' Satan's whiskey"—that's what I told her. And once in Carter's store they had that candy kiss, you know? "Oh, candy tastes better'n kissin' and huggin' and suckin' our necks." I tol' ol' Morris that. But I'm no drunker. Only once and that was when my sister's husband held me down, and she pressed the little spot on my head where my ol' drunker-mother always beat me with stove-wood, and it got bright and bright and then I passed out and they poured ol' Satan's whiskey down me. He was the same one who followed me up Carter's hill blackberry-pickin', but that was a while back. He's got children by my sister now, and he still drinks.

9

We, the Wilderness

Honest, Jesus does talk to me, every night. When I go to bed I hear him say to pray as usual. "You pray as usual Letty, you pray the right way for every person in the world." I always try to make it good for all us Indian people, but you know one person I been scared of, it's not Jesus, it's that ol' Janet. "Get out of here, get out of here! You don't belong here!" She said that. "Oh, shut your mouth there's just one Lord God for us all!" I said that back. That was when her drunker-sister turned colors and died, and them partyin' 'round that purple body, her and Kaleb, why they hadn't even called the preacher in! So when they brought that boy in I started prayin' my war prayer and hymnin' for the sailors and their children. Then when she unlocked the door to let us in I felt it comin': "Guard the sailors tossin' on the deep blue sea." I prayed and woke up hearin' myself prayin', "Precious Jesus!" Hearin', while she talked so stern and storm-like, the calm whisper: "Grant to little children visions bright of Thee," only it was like the calm before a storm, flat-calm. I heard it comin' while she led us down the hall and in his room, the nurses passin' him like little puffs of wind, and when I sat down on the chair and touched that spot, scratchin' my scalp like so nobody would notice, holdin' to the bedpost as the room began to spin and gettin' bright and bright his white sheets and the nurses nearly caught up with him, reelin' like they're drunk on Jesus' wine. Honest I really did see somethin', call it a whirlwind, movin' 'round and pickin' people up—Dean this time, Hazen later, never miss a one—movin' all us people somewheres else away from here. And some seemed happy flyin' in that funnel like my ol' ghost-granny or an angel maybe, while the others looked distempered and all splotchy like a salmon when he starts to go upstream to where he come from. But nobody come back from that whirlwind, it passed on by. Maybe it rained somewhere else, I don't know, but not here, 'cause I woke up then and found myself prayin' for everyone of us who has to die.

Lydia

At first I was glad to be on duty: it had happened, he had done it and it couldn't be undone; I hadn't been there to prevent him but I was beside him now, could help him, could *do something*. That was always the most frustrating, no matter what you felt, you didn't dare *do* anything, it might be misinterpreted. Now I could do, must do, they expected it of me—hold his hand or check the instruments or *something*. It was awful though watching him suffer, and I had to pretend he was a stranger, a patient, every time the needle on the cardiograph wavered.

Then *they* came in, dressed all in black (just raincoats, but the way they wore them, walked, and sat down heavily, reminded me of ravens) and I knew before it happened, and they knew I knew, that if I was an angel of mercy they were the death-angel and their medicine was older and stronger. He sensed it too, their presence, though he couldn't see them sitting, and if I were back in school now speaking to a group of student-nurses about Patient X and the effects on his pulse-rate induced by visits of his blood-kin, I would say it was most interesting. I felt bewitched, or in the presence of bewitching; while they hovered and the needle on the cardiograph wavered, I felt like yelling "Murderers!" and driving them with respirator-cords out of the room. Yet I was held too, helpless, like a paper-doll (I don't know how better to put it), my neck flushed and stinging as though chafed by raw weather. And when one of them reached out to touch the corner of the bedpost—I was holding Dean's wrist limply in my hand, counting his pulse—I felt the shock, electric, and a shudder like slow thunder roll through him. Then he began to bleed through the bedsheet.

I ran into the hall. By the door where he was talking, Kaleb nodded slow and grave. The doctor saw me then and moved that nervous chain-smoke way he has of moving, darting past like air or smoke that never settles. Marge went in with the doctor so I stayed out, busying my hands like I was faint. I smoothed my dress or patted my hair, did something, anything, and knew my face and neck were flushed for I felt nauseous. Kaleb didn't move and then he did, slowly, and I could see he knew already and was dreading to go in because the others might expect him to say something. He didn't know what he could say and stopped beside me pleading with his eyes, but very masculine, and I was pleading too in my own way. And then he touched me, just reached and touched my hand, but firm and steady and I knew his grief was greater than mine was or ever could be—mute, inarticulate, but great: more than a person mourning for a person, he was a people mourning a lost past. I couldn't cry—how could I? I hadn't any right. His firm hand turned me gently and I let him usher me into the room where, the respirator gone now, Dean was gasping wildly for his breath, his eyes wide open.

Kaleb walked slowly, very slowly, to the bed and took his hand. You could see Dean's body, his whole body gather to respond, as though the slightest pressure on his palm shocked him all over, and he couldn't figure out where it came from. Then he did. Suddenly his eyes focused on Kaleb, he gripped his hand and gasped, "I'm . . sor . ry . . . Dad . . . ." and waited. Kaleb started to say something while Dean waited, we all waited, but the words, if there were ever any words, got stuck or frightened and Aunt Janet from the far side grabbed Dean's other hand and broke in, "It's all right, Dean, it's all right, we forgive you, dear, it's all right," while his father stood there sweating and Dean bleeding through the bedsheet.

BOOK ONE

Dean
Doctor Sharp

Dean

Swimming underwater in a deep sea-weed green room, with Lydia, and breathing was no problem. I would kick from the stomach and glide lithely down to her, but she was shy and would not come with me. Her red hair waving slowly like grass in a current, while her white limbs flashed quicksilver like fish-schools, now waiting, baiting, now running—she in virgin flight, I in germinal pursuit—only we were children and the chase would never end. Then she turned to touch me on my quick of pleasure, trick me, and I tried to surface but couldn't. The air went out of me, escaping at my prick, and she held me down by holding her hand there. I watch, astonished, as her hand turns brown and as the dirty color travels up her arm and down her body. She is brown now, Indian like me and laughing at me, older than I am, and terrible. She pulls me towards and into her, my pleasure-point first and then the rest of me collapsing, drawn into her narrow whirlpool hole. She is the water now, the murky and dark water. I am drowning. . . .

Because it's like that when you live your whole life on the ocean, and half the people you have ever known have drowned, most of them twice: drowned the mind first with liquor, then fallen overboard to drown the body. And why not? You watch the porpoise wheeling and the killer-whales finning, even the sea-lions, massy-fat and scarlet in the sun, are freer than you are; and if it weren't for the little boy they recovered at Blind Channel, the one the older kids pushed off the dock, if you

15

hadn't seen his face suckered with starfish, you'd likely have gone swimming long ago. Because it's like that when you live on a small island and can't leave it: the ocean surrounds your conscious mind. It undermines and eventually it overcomes it; so it's merely a question of time, more or less, a question of timing, now or later. Only now means a decision, and what's there to decide when the pros and cons are all mixed up? The tide flows in and the tide flows out, the ocean leaves its droppings at your doorstep—strange wares and wishbones of the drowned; but it will return to take your garbage, and what today did not bring you, tomorrow may, and what tomorrow takes away is yours today, and there is nothing you can do to stop the tides or stay the flood since you are here today and gone tomorrow anyway, and who cares why? The mind is governed by the tides, the old ones say, the tides are governed by the moon; the moon is governed by the sun, which never shines, for the sun is governed by no one. Thinking, maybe we are not God's children after all, maybe we are just God's salmon, spawn; and the Fisher has beguiled us into thinking we are free, that though He kills us it is we who kill ourselves, though we die we live forever in His stomach.

I twist slightly, agonizingly. The pit of my stomach is on fire. A hand is on my brow. I smell Lydia, her sweat through the perfume she always wears. I must touch her. "Lydia," I say, but hear nothing. I try again. This time she draws her hand from off my brow.

"Shhh," she whispers, and lays her finger on my lips.

That was the amazing thing: nothing had changed. The tide had shifted, that was all. The worst of it was I had killed the body first, whereas everybody I had ever known killed the mind and let others see to the disposing of their body. Worse luck, that due to mechanical failures I had gummed the works. At least Danny hadn't blown the attempt. When they put *him* on the stretcher it was only him from the neck down—his mind was blown, spattered all over the basement ceiling. Lydia had cried too, even though she hadn't known Danny that well. She was with him just before he did it and she cried, I saw her, the next night:

"Why are you drunk? My God! Why are you drinking?" Her smell was fresh like she'd just bathed. Standing in the doorway of the nurses' residence, that blue gown, when the light was right behind it, you could see through; standing with the light behind her, in the door. "Wasn't Danny's death enough? Why do you do it?"

"I want to leave this place," I said, "I want to go."

"No," she said, "it's because your mother left you, it's because *she* committed suicide, that's why you come here. Here. . . ." and she took my hand and laid it on her breast inside the gown. "This is what you want, need; but I'm a nurse, not a nurse-maid." Then she was gone, a finger on her lips as if to say, "Tell no one, not even yourself. Do not remember tomorrow what I have done tonight."

And the next morning she stepped over me—me drunk on the boardwalk—on her brittle click-clack way to the hospital.

I ought to call her just for spite, just lift the bell and she'd come running, not stepping over now, she couldn't now that I'm a patient and helpless, she couldn't step over. But would she come because I'd called her, or because I am a patient and helpless? I can't be sure. I never could be sure why, as I lay a child alone in my own bed, why in the middle of the night sometimes my mother came and slept with me. I'd wished it so and whispered for her: was that the reason? And after mother left and I lay night after night wishing she'd come back, one night, the first I can remember, my sister Laverne came (looking even then just like mother, only thinner; that was before Laverne had Michael) and sat down on the bed and took my hand and held it a long time, a long time sitting saying nothing, then, "You miss her." While I looked terrified and pleading up at her, terrified she might leave too, until she let out a deep breath and pulled back the covers and scrunched in next to me and went to sleep. And I lay there quiet, happy, hardly breathing, hearing father's snoring from the kitchen through the door.

It was like that, then, until I was thirteen. Laverne got married then; she was fifteen. Before it happened there were whole nights she was gone. She would come to bed early and then slip out as soon as father started snoring, until after a while, when she and Hazen were engaged, she didn't bother coming in at all. She was getting ready to leave me, I knew it, then she left. But after she'd had Michael they came back. Hazen built a little room onto the back and they moved up from the beachhouse, so Laverne could do the cooking and take care of grandpa.

That made six of us counting Hazen, plus the kids: Grandpa Gideon, father, Uncle Josh who'd never married and who sold pop, chips, and candy from the front part of the house, me, Louisa and baby Michael, with Hazen and Laverne in the back room. That was after my great-aunt Margaret died and there wasn't anyone to do the cooking, and we got tired of going down to Aunt Janet's for supper. So Laverne, she was eighteen now and a mother, did the cooking and it was "sure nice to have a woman round the house again," as Uncle Josh said, "even if it does mean walk on tiptoe and don't spit." It sure was. "Cause it kinder gives the place a center," as Josh put it. Only where before there was no center since mother left the house, now again, as when she'd been there, there were two.

You had to walk around on tiptoe so the baking wouldn't fall and the baby wouldn't wake and that was one center, the kitchen, where you came in and sat down and ate and talked and lived (where Grandpa Gideon slept, too, all day). Or you could lie awake at night and listen for the other, the night-scent and secret of the house now a woman was around again; listen, scarcely breathing, for the muffled woman sounds (between your father's snoring), the message in the rain on the tin roof of the back porch, the woodshed Hazen built without a door. It had a bed though, that other center, and you lay awake at night scarcely breathing, listening, and knew your Uncle Josh in the next room was listening too, as he had before, when there had been a woman in the house, before you were, when he lay in the bed where you now lay, and she lay in the bed where he now lay, and your father in the place he'd always lay snored as he always had. You knew that too, as surely as you knew old Josh had always listened.

So you'd lay awake listening to a new place which the ear and the house were not yet accustomed to, hearing though the old familiar secret sound—you'd hear it and you'd wonder if Josh did. Then next morning he'd say, "Better have *three* eggs, boy," to Hazen, and wink at him, and Hazen would look stupid, then a sheepish grin would sugar-coat his face and Laverne would whirl around from the cookstove—it was the silence following, not the remark; it was Hazen's dumbness that ired her —glaring, and hiss like steam off the hot oven, brandishing the poker in her hand: "You stuu-pid!" While the grin on Hazen's face would run like icing off a hotcake because he knew, we all knew, there would be no more night sounds for a full week.

Hazen took great pains not to get tricked again, and he didn't, until last week. It was the day before Glenn Elkin's wedding, and Josh said to Kaleb (he was Glenn's best man), "Make sure you got the ring, now, Kale. Don't want it to be like old Chief Harris' wedding."

Hearing a joke coming, father smiled and sipped his coffee. "How was that?" he asked politely.

"Well, when they got to the ring part," Josh said, addressing Hazen and me now, "the best man found he didn't have it. He figured the old Chief must have it on him, so he signalled him like this"—into a thumb-and-finger-hole Josh poked his middle finger, in and out. Hazen watched fascinated. Josh glanced covertly at Laverne's back at the stove, then continued, "But the old Chief had only one thing on his mind. 'Later,' he said, so loud the people heard him. 'Laa-ter!' " Josh repeated it with relish, illustrating as for an idiot with finger-play, while watching out of the corner of his eye Laverne's back stiffen. Father and I watched Hazen's broad face broaden: he hadn't quite caught it, but he would. Laverne waited a full ten-second count before turning to survey Hazen's moon-face. She didn't even say stuu-pid, just glared, then turned and left the kitchen. Hazen withered. "And tonight a wedding-night," Josh remarked innocently. "She's just like her mother," Father said.

In the evening Josh got Hazen drunk, which didn't happen often, although Josh fell off the wagon pretty regularly each month when the month-end store accounts came due, and father was an every week-end drinker. Grandpa Gideon kept their bottles stashed away and on request he'd pad into the pantry and get one, muttering and shaking his head about how times had changed when the only change, according to father, was that Grandpa Gideon couldn't hold his anymore. "Oh, it's true they didn't drink," father admitted to me once, "they ate Indian-root and got diarrhea and visions and danced and called it all religion. Now the white man takes our drugs and goes fishing on weekends, while we drink his booze and go to church. And who can say who got the worst of it, hmm? who can say?"

So Glenn's was a church-wedding and the liquor flowed; it started flowing that afternoon, Friday, and it was still flowing Sunday night. Hazen came home Friday night late (Josh put him up to it) and tried to crawl in with Laverne, but she kicked him out and locked the door. Then Saturday just after Grandpa Gideon and I had finished supper Hazen came, unshaved but sober (Josh and Father were still partying some place), and persuaded Laverne to go with him to Glenn's place, while I watched baby Michael. She was home before midnight and locked the door, said Hazen had got stoned and lost his teeth and was crawling around under the furniture at Glennie's looking for them. She laughed that throaty laugh she does when she feels good and went to bed—she'd had a few herself—and I remember thinking to myself how ridiculous it was to get married: that here Laverne was feeling good and bedding down alone, and there was Hazen searching for his teeth. Then baby Michael woke up crying and, of course, there was the reason. She got up and passed my bed on her way to the kitchen. On her way back I stirred and she hesitated slightly as though she had forgotten something and was trying to remember, but couldn't quite, and wanted to ask someone but couldn't think of what to ask. She went on and I heard her sitting on the bedside a long time before getting in, and I lay in bed a long time before getting up and going in, but finally I did go in. There was one little window and it wasn't raining out but the moon rode low and was low behind the mountain so it was pitch-dark in the room and I was glad. A strong cedar odor off the shakes mingled with the woman-smell she gave off, and I remembered it had been her period before this spat with Hazen (Josh, at breakfast, likening this latest shut-out to Hazen's losing a world series double-header). I sat down on the bed and said nothing, just stared out the window; after all, I had nothing to say, or so much I wouldn't know where to begin. Questions: about our mother, maybe, why she'd left us? Laverne was older, might remember something, some clue maybe . . . but she wouldn't know, anymore than I. Or about us, she and I, why we never talked to one another anymore; why everything, if there was anything between us, must go unspoken, be forgotten, lost. Why we were dying—Father, Hazen tonight and Josh forever, she and I—drinking ourselves into oblivion and dying, crying and afraid to cry out or reach out—who could we cry to? what could we cling to? what could we say to one another? . . .

nothing . . . no one. . . . When she took my hand, and the vast
unspoken past welled up in me—I cried, I couldn't help it—and
she drew me down to cry into her breasts.

After a while it was all over and I lay there while she patted my back softly, saying, "It's all right now, it's all right, isn't
it?" I nodded, nudging the softness that was her now, but long
ago was someone else, and later on would be someone else
again; nudging her and feeling her hand stop and knowing that
already it was different between us than it had been, that lying
there my face upon her breast was different than it had been
only an instant earlier: though we had not either of us moved
or spoken and were exactly the same persons we had been, lying
in the same place, in the same house, yet different, changed,
each waiting for the other to make some move, speak some
word, for it was all unspoken still and even in that moment our
two lonelinesses had not touched. Afraid to move or speak we
lay there, her hand resting on my back, my head buried in her
breasts, until we both grew warm and slick with sweat and I
drew upward and lay down beside her on the bed, in Hazen's
place. She didn't draw the covers up or close her gown at once,
she turned her head on the pillow and looked at me (she was
lying on her back, I on my side, facing her)—a prolonged gazing
at my face as though for the first and the last time—then turned
onto her side away from me the way she always used to sleep
in years long past. Only it wasn't the same now, I knew it and
she knew it, and though I lay a long time trying to convince
myself it was, then trying to decide to get up and go back to my
own bed, then trying just to fall asleep, I guess she knew I
wouldn't but wanted me to try, wanted to try herself maybe,
before, by the time it started raining, she turned over on her
back and drew me to her.

She made no sound. The rain from drizzle and catsfeet beginnings swelled and burst and in that instant she had thrust
her arms to me and drawn me to her. All the armies of the

world marched on our roof yet we were safe. I had the strange sensation, though, just as she guided me in her and locked her legs around my hips and with one hand drew and held me against her and with the other continued to excite me, the strange sensation I was part of a whirlpool. The planes and angles of our bodies lost all certain definition, the softness of her breasts seemed part of me, and the hardness of my tool a part of her. She was all around me, both above and beneath me, drawing me down to her, thrusting me away, over; now she was above me leaning down and drawing my mouth up as if for air. I was a part of the cedar-smelling water and swelling, or being sucked, up or down I wasn't sure but deep and sudden and it seemed the instant that the water released me, the moment I came gasping up for breath—still surrounded by the water but on its surface spent and gasping—it seemed the whirlpool which had drawn me down and flung me up had sunk or spent itself just like the rain. There was not an eddy on the surface, not a tremor in that body of white-water, not a twitch. I lay off to one side a little shaken, thinking somehow I had got out on the wrong side of the river and sometime, tomorrow, or the next day, or the next, I would have to cross back over to get out.

But there wasn't a tomorrow. Danny killed himself that night. When I heard it I knew there could be no going back, I would have to stay on the side of the river I was on. Laverne knew too, though probably she never thought of it that way, that this act or that decision mattered or could change you. Father said once she was like mother in thinking we were Indians and that was that. "Indians being to your mother, and your sister too, the race God started with but left behind with Nature, the people told to hide and watch from behind trees the white and yellow and black men make history."

"Why, aren't we part of history?" I asked him.

"No," he said, "we never have been. We are subject to it,

but not part of it. We watch the others, that is all. It may be
when the rest have learned what we never questioned, or failed
to learn it, we may be the last men too." Laverne probably never worried about what we'd done; she probably never thought
of it as having crossed a river. She was the river, after all. Maybe
she had crossed some other river earlier, the thought struck me,
or maybe just being born an Indian was to have been dropped
on the wrong side, maybe she thought that way. Or maybe, and
it came to me that morning as Hazen told us about Danny,
maybe what they meant, she and my mother, was there wasn't
any river to cross over or, rather, no dry ground to stand on,
none at all. And if there wasn't any river to cross and no ground
to stand on, how could there be a wrong side or a right? If all
was water then you either swam or sank, and since it was in
your nature to do both it was merely a question of time, more
or less, a question of timing, now or later.

That came to me as Hazen told us about Danny—talking
like a man with oatmeal in his mouth and his lip where it'd
been split a little swollen—sitting talking to Laverne's back at
the stove and my face across the kitchen table and Grandpa
Gideon's bald head nodding yes, yes, in the kind of chant he
used to do at Pentecostal meetings, till the warm room and the
early hour and the length of Hazen's tale conspired against the
old man and his rheumy lidless eyes fluttered a little and
squeezed shut and the slowly nodding head started once then
came to rest on the out-thrust collar-bone age had provided as
a perch. Over Father's slack-jawed snoring from the corner and
baby Michael's outbursts of delight at the texture and tied-on-
ness of my buttons, Hazen told us, told us about Danny. While
I watched Laverne grow tired with the telling, and Grandpa
Gideon nod off, and Father snore, and Hazen, who was there
when it happened relieve himself with telling it now he was
home; while I sat listening, hearing the story of another which
is now my own, hearing clearly and distinctly as though a spirit

spoke the pronouncement of the doom laid on us all—though only I heard it, and Danny. . . .

Danny had heard it and he'd jumped off the boat where a bunch of them were drinking, Hazen said, and started swimming, ". . . like a guy when he's been drinking and gets somethin' in his head and thinks it's somewhere else and starts out for it—only there was nothin' out there, only water." By the time they weighed anchor and pulled up alongside he was a long way out towards the straits beside Grave Island.

"If he'd ever got in there," Hazen said, "he'd been a goner, even if he was a strong swimmer." They came up alongside, but he veered away, so they came along again and tossed the line, but he kept swimming. Finally they had to hook his jacket with the gaff and haul him in, him struggling and yelling, "Lemme go, don't make me come back, lemme go!"

"And he wadn't drunk," mused Hazen softly like an old man, as though without his teeth he couldn't quite digest the matter, "he wadn't drunk at all, though he'd been drinkin'." They got him in, and dried him out, and passed it off, or tried to; everybody had a drink and Danny admitted it was foolish to go swimming off a boat that time of night above the straits, he admitted it was certain suicide and they all laughed and drank to that and said it looked like you was swimming to Grave Island, and laughed again, and he said promise me you won't go telling anyone I tried and didn't do it, and they said hell no, you were just out swimming, Danny, in the moonlight, and Hazen said you just fell off the boat, you drunk, and Danny hit him in the mouth once, hard, and split the lip a little but not badly since his teeth weren't in. Then Danny picked him up and said he was sorry and offered to let Hazen hit him back, and Hazen swung and missed, and Danny said again don't go telling anyone and left the boat. He went up to the nurses' residence then, Hazen said: ". . . he was thick on that Lydia-nurse, you know." And after that he went to see his granny Phereba.

"She was comin' up the boardwalk as I come," Hazen continued, "about a hundred of her family around her, I had to wait. That sure is a big family." Laverne sat down from tiredness and stared at baby Michael. "Go on," she said flatly.

"Well, it was in that basement room, 'round three, four o'clock. They never even heard the shot upstairs. Old Dan was passed out, Vina too, I guess; the littlest one says she heard somethin' and cried awhile but when nobody got up, she went back to sleep. I was sleepin' on the boat when Doctor Sharp sent down for guys to help him with the body. When I heard it was Danny I hightailed home." Laverne stared wearily while Father snored, and Grandpa Gideon, I will say this for him, slept quietly. The baby had dropped off too, lulled by Hazen's voice.

"Well . . .?" Hazen said, looking from Laverne to me and back again. "Well, what a family this is! Everybody flaked out, and old Josh passed out too on the boardwalk, righten th' rain." Laverne's stare flickered briefly, enough to wither Hazen—"I didn't mean nothin'," he recanted quickly—but not deigning to reply, she stared down again. I eased Michael off my lap onto Laverne's.

"About how long ago did Doctor Sharp send down?" I asked.

" 'Bout as long's it takes a hundred people to pass you on the boardwalk," he replied, quick and grateful for the question, not even asking why I'd asked it; then, "That sure is a big family, and Danny the brightest of the lot. A guy can't help but wonder why he did it, why anybody'd do a thing like that. Where ya goin'?"

"Over to find out, I guess," I said, and left him to mull that without his teeth.

I was pretty sure I knew, but hoped I didn't. For the mind is quicker than the trigger-finger, father said. "Or the fingerprint," Josh added, "in the vaseline jar." I was pretty sure I knew but if I did why didn't Hazen, and Josh passed out on the boardwalk, and Father snoring in the kitchen, and Danny's father Dan passed out in bed? Why did they all plead ignorance? Why, Josh and Father, Dan too, didn't even know Danny was dead. Which means they weren't expecting it. So maybe I was wrong, maybe there *was* some reason peculiar to Danny, some little quirk which came as a surprise even to him. And if there was, it was worth finding out—not for Danny's sake, but for my own.

There was quite a crowd outside the basement door, young men and boys, waiting. Then Doctor Sharp arrived with the stretcher and signalled three or four to come in with him. We went through the basement to the little corner room where Vina, Danny's stepmother, stacked cardboard boxes for burning (she kept a house-front store like Uncle Josh). Doctor Sharp opened the door onto the little room and at first all you could see were cardboard boxes, piled high and flecked with what first looked like confetti or Christmas spray. Then the two guys in front began to puke and came out with their hands over their mouths and you saw Danny, lying on the floor between the boxes like a river running through a mountain-gorge—the floor so wet, and *sticky*. That was what had turned the first two: they'd stepped in him and he'd stuck. That, and the white bits of bone, and brain, and the blood splattered on the boxes and the ceiling. It was rough, rough enough to give you the cold chills, especially when we rolled him onto the stretcher and a big part of his head stuck to the floor. He was just meat. It wasn't like he was a person, or human even, just cold stiff meat. Certainly his Indianness didn't matter now, or whatever other petty quirk short-circuited the mind and made the trigger-finger quicker. Doctor Sharp said not to touch the shotgun, so we left it. I remember wondering would the old folks put the gun on Danny's grave, the way they did favorite possessions; or would they in bewilderment and grief blame the gun, as they blamed the ocean for drownings, and whiskey for drunkenness, and basketball for pregnancies? Then we brought the stretcher out, completely sheeted, through the crowd, and the men looked glum as weather and stared down, while the women started wailing from the house.

We maneuvered the wet boardwalk with extreme care, Doctor Sharp stopping abruptly and jerking round so often to make sure we hadn't dropped it that we nearly tripped on him and almost did. Then we turned onto the main boardwalk and he walked alongside, anxious and concerned as though it was a patient we carried and not a corpse. I was on the outside, towards the water, and between beach-houses and through stilts I watched a freight-train bear down on the village then swing out away from shore and down the Straits. Seattle-bound, down from Alaska: from Ketchikan, or Juneau, or who knows, maybe Inuvik. A hundred barges passed us everyday, carrying from Nome to Frisco, from Seattle to Juneau (or maybe just Vancouver to Prince Rupert), trains, grains, trucks, troops, houses and house-trailers. A hundred barges day and night slid by us without blowing even; or sometimes in the night when there was fog you'd hear the whistle, urgent, shrill, and think a train was coming, and it might be, but the tug would turn out to the lighthouse and its foghorn, booming steady and so natural you'd never hear it, would answer and guide safely past the rocks and shallows and the sleeping Indians both tug and train. Or sometimes, when the ocean liner passed by at night so fast and with such draft its wake sounds like surf pounding for an hour, the guys would have to get up and go down and pump their boats out. Only once did a boat stop besides the fishboats, and that was when that big U.S. troop carrier hit a rock and there was weather and the sailors were all billeted in the village. No weddings came of it but lots of family and a few songs and lots of fighting. The world paid us one visit, anyway.

I remember watching that train, wondering if it's going

anywhere, anywhere worth going, worth hopping a ride to any destination, destiny; or is it just one more interminable trip back and forth like a stretcher-case to the hospital for repairs . . . only this time it's a corpse, though no one can see that beneath the sheet, but they all know. . . .

We marched on to the hospital, on through the hospital, marching across water to Grave Island. There was no fixing up to do—closed coffin. A nurse was holding the door open, not Lydia. Then, behind us, just the slightest little gasp and the doctor, flustered, saying, "Yes, it's him, yes, I'm sorry, Miss Archer, terribly sorry, excuse me. . . ." And as I turned backwards to take the stretcher through the door I saw her standing, a house-robe thrown around her and her hair mussed with the print of sleep still on her face, looking quizzical, surprised, somehow betrayed.

It's her night-self, I told myself, I've never seen before; I've only seen her day-face and starched uniform and hair up in a bun, but this is her night-self, that Danny saw. And watching the sleep fade from her face and the features sharpen, tighten underneath that red luxuriance of hair, the odd curler dangling like a trophy or a beaver-claw left in the trap, I knew before it happened, before she fixed me with a look and reached and pulled the sheet back and the doctor pivoted as neatly as you please and puked on the radiator, that whatever petty guilts they might try to hang it on—family problems, Danny's step-mother, his quitting school, the income tax he owed—here was the real reason, vivid, secret, personal, but not peculiar to Danny, no, not to him alone. I knew that too, and had a feeling as I reached to pull the sheet back that I was reaching for one of those flashbulb tourist-boats, the liner white and sparkling sliding thirty knots down channel . . . reaching . . . but it was night already and a freight-train from the straits hit me instead and shoved me reeling down a whirlpool straight to hell . . .

Doctor Sharp

Since Danny, I'd given it a lot of thought and decided it was sheer recurrence, not clairvoyance. When those painted finger-nails in the name of peace pulled back that sheet I saw no single face—no face at all, in fact—but several: beginning not with Danny's and not ending with his either, nor with Dean's; but stretching back before their births and on beyond their passing into the has-been and the not-yet like a single shrill inhuman scream, a shriek of horror or revulsion such as Kali of the severed heads and flashing feet and painted finger- and toe-nails might make if she were not insatiable and foreign. If she were not the red bitch-goddess men make her. In their myths they call woman "Peacemaker"; man makes war. They omit to men-tion that he battles to obtain, then to retain, his precious peace. Woman the peacemaker, the prize, whose present of herself commences war. It was all there: the prize, the slain young war-rior, the price, the field of blood, and the embattled (one won-ders?) virginity. A gesture in the name of hope, a look of helplessness, and enter the lists a new and foredoomed victim, victim to the old predestined lust. It was all there, the makings of a re-run melodrama like the last act of a medieval miracle play but without the miracle; only the slaughter, over and over, the tragedy oft repeated become comedy, but worse . . . because you know this comedy will never end and the laugh you counted on relieving you gets stuck in your craw and you won't have it, no one will if you see another victim because there won't be any actors left on stage. There won't even be an audience, only that single shrill inhuman scream, that chilling laugh at all the fools who staked their lives upon a play, a miracle, whether of Medicine or God, a happy ending. That was when I turned to laugh and vomited instead.

When they carried what was Danny on in through the door, and while I stood there fiddling with the radiator, trying to shut it off to ease the smell, Lydia took over. She wasn't even on duty. The nurse on duty was new, and stood in the hallway astonished as beslippered and house-robed, red hair in curlers, Lydia directed the stretcher into emergency and helped Dean pour Danny out onto the slab. Well, it was fitting: the virago laying out her victim with her future victim's aid; a dress-rehearsal, and only she would be around for the curtain, the last laugh, only she knew that the play was not make-believe. I had the numbing feeling I had seen it all before, but it seemed real enough stitching Danny's death-masque, and breaking the news to his father when he came to that afternoon, and sedating old Phereba the grandmother when the women wailing gave her palpitations and her heart stopped. Letty and that Pentecostal bunch of hangers-on—ghoulish, I'd call them. It was real, but I was certain I had seen it all before. What with the crowd scenes, the professional mourners, and the extras—old Battleaxe Beatrice who scrubbed the blood off the walls, and Fat Maggie who moved in to do the food—it was turning into a production, with the pay-off on the night after the funeral, the feast, where Fat Maggie and B.B. and the wailers and the prayers and the watchers and the burners and the diggers and the Doctor (yes, the doctor too) got theirs in blankets and a tidbit of cash too from the family, the weary woe-begotten family; while the family, doling gratuities and gifts and foodstuffs out one door, received donations in another (of a dollar, or a dollar and a half) from members of the family once removed and sympathizers, mainly those who'd had a recent death in their own family and

knew a cast of thousands was involved. The surprise came when
they heaped up blankets on Vina and kept on heaping them—
on the table in front, and on her lap, and then beside and all
around her—as though to suffocate her as she sat in the warm
room rigid and immobile and unsweating, her hard eyes staring
straight ahead, unblinking. She was Danny's stepmother and
from another tribe; she was younger than old Dan and she and
Danny had been overheard to quarrel about the store she ran,
and money matters. She was pretty too, in a hard way, much
too attractive for old Dan. So having fixed the blame the family
now proceeded to shame her Indian-style. Old Dan the father
could do nothing; he sat beside her dull-eyed, dumb, his great
loose features dripping sweat as though he had been drinking,
while the old women, his sisters and his aunts and his first
wife's mother and her daughters, wordlessly heaped gifts and
guilt on Vina, literally buried her in blankets. She bore it, all
their crochet-work and xenophobia, bore it without ever batting
an eyelash or fidgeting a finger or relinquishing a single drop of
sweat. I suppose she switched on some schizoid frequency and
just detached, "went Indian" they call it, the way Lydia pre-
tended Danny's death was make-believe—women have a faculty
for that.

  With me it was more difficult, I didn't agonize and anguish
like Old Dan (he wasn't the same after; always wearing that
slack-jowled expression like a mask and seeming always on the
verge of crying or of ripping off his clothes to show you the
invisible stigmata: "See, this proves it, they were wrong!
It was *me, my* mistakes he died for; my shame she suffered
and endures!"). Poor bastard. With me it required a lot
of introspection to admit that, whatever ignominious illogic they
might use to justify themselves, the women in the long run were
correct. The more you pondered it—not just Danny's, but the
spate of suicides his was one digit in, and the reasons or utter
lack of them—the more you realized here was no simple murder-

mystery with clues and motives and a discernible villain. You
had your victims plain enough, this year's crop at least, Danny
and Dean, and you had this year's villainess, Lydia; while Vina
took the rap for her—both unaware: the one that she was cul-
pable, the other that she wasn't. But what of next year's batch,
and after? of last year's, and before? None of the same people
were involved, or would be. The "heavies," who weren't really
heavy, had as rapid a turnover as the innocents, not really in-
nocent. Lydia, given a new year and a new cast, will likely
marry some nice Indian who'll get drunk every night and beat
her up; while Dean and Danny will be nestled snug and peaceful with their mothers (who also committed suicide) on Grave
Island. So where's injustice? Each one gets his heart's desire
and probably his due, too, in the end. And yet, while this year's
stage is bare, the season ended, next year's is already being cast:
the play endures, like that single stark misshapen maple tree,
blighted and dying, which sheds fewer leaves each fall but still
litters the boardwalk and hospital grounds with splendid scarlets
and yellows, purples, mauves and browns, more lavish in senil-
ity than youth.

That is why I love the Indian people and culture. Misshapen maybe and axe-ringed a hundred years ago as though it
was a wolf-tree to be cleared, not fit for marketing, to make way
for progress and for tree-farm saplings uniform in height, type,
growth, mechanically planted, graded, harvested. But they endured. They endured by virtue of not being marketable, by dint
of not competing, by receding and withdrawing—into older
woods, or onto remote islands. Only the women weren't con-
tent to just withdraw; they followed, but halfheartedly, back-
glancing Lot's-wifelike. And there were always those who
sought them out—traders, missionaries, government agents;
miners, loggers, fishermen—always men. And the Indian women
who resented the withdrawal, not the geographical hardship
but what it told them of their men, the fear they smelled upon

them as they lay with them at night; the women, maybe out of curiosity, received into their island strongholds, into the impregnable positions they had fled to—miners, loggers, fishermen; traders, missionaries, agents—anyone who dared to track them there, for God or Company or, later, from boredom—trophy-hunters, tourists, college drop-outs turned hippy; and, oh yes, doctors: missionary-doctors and anthropologists. They received them all, all men. And if their men waited in ambush, or got drunk and went berserk, they ran out to warn the stranger, ran away with him, only to come dragging back big-bellied or aborted. They received the white intruder into their island hideout, ancient longhouse, welfare home, into their primeval female cave . . . and gradually their men gave up.

That is what I came to, sitting in Old Dan's house hearing the low certain drone of women in command dispersing gifts; studying their faces and the faces of the men like little boys waiting, not resentful but patient, waiting to receive a gift to recompense them somewhat for the right of which they'd been deprived—their pride of manhood. Thinking, they have lost their land and the reason for the land, their women; now they lose their life.

It all seemed very logical and, from where I sat, digesting a big Indian meal prepared by Indian women, letting their slow Indian drone roll over and drug me, verifiable as well. Wasn't the proof there in Mona Matson, warm and brown, a trace of perspiration where she carried the blankets when the older women called the winning name? The same Mona, nurses' aid, who at a staff party five years ago, giggly and even warmer after a few drinks, surprised me when I sneaked out once Old Bell the minister took over—fielding hymn-requests while his wife played her accordion— by jumping from behind my bedroom door, flipping off the light and giggling, "Peekaboo! Guess who?"

"I haven't the slightest idea," I said.

"She's brown all over, furry in spots, and burrows like a little mouse—if you'll let her." And to illustrate this last she dug her nose into my back.

"Ouch!" I said, and switched on the bedlamp.

"It's your lil' ol' Mona," she said sulkily.

"So it is. I was just about to read," I said, and sat down on the bed. She sat down too. "Where is Freddy?"

"Oh, he's ol' passed out," she pouted.

"Passed out? On what? Hymn-singing?"

"Silly. In the kitchen. Andy brought some stuff in through your window." Then, "He used the ladder."

"Oh."

"You don't mind?"

"No. Of course not."

"Roger," she leaned into me and caught hold of my arm, "you doan' mind if I call you Roger? I've had five babies," holding up one hand and counting, "four by Freddy," thumb down, counting again, "but Freddy is the biggest baby of the lot. Roger. . . ."

I had a hard time getting rid of her. She wanted an examination, she said finally, and hiked her skirt up. I stood up about as quickly as I could and fumbled for a cigarette. "I haven't the proper equipment here," I said.

She giggled and fell back across the bed. "Ro-*jer*," she said.

I did the only thing I could in the circumstances, switched the ceiling light on. "If you'll come to my office tomorrow at, say, three. . . ."

The light did it. She straightened at her skirt and sort of rolled onto one elbow. "You're altogether different from your father," she said.

"How do you mean?"

"Oh, never mind. You better do your reading, Doctor." She stood up.

"What did you mean about my father?" I demanded.

"Nothing," she repeated, giggling, "not a thing. I guess I've had a few." Then, worried, "You won't tell Freddy I came, will you? He'd beat me—he would, too! He does that—oh, he's such an ox!"

"I won't tell him," I promised, and thanked my lucky stars she wouldn't either.

It was immediately after, as Mona and I emerged from the hallway trying to look inconspicuous, that Old Bell the minister caught sight of me and shouted: "Roger! hold on. For he's a jolly good fellow, folks!" And I had to stand and take it. Then a birthday or some kind of cake came out and he announced: "Tonight, folks, is a very special occasion. Roger's wedding anniversary, you might say. Ten years married to the village of Nanootkish, in sickness and in health, and let us hope," his voice lapsing off into that tone ministers use, "till death do thee part." He laughed at his own joke then led everyone in singing

> *I want a gur-rul*
> *just like the girl*
> *that married dear old Dad.*
>
> *She was a pur-rul*
> *and the only girl*
> *that Dad-dee ev-ver had. . . .*

And while we munched cake (Mona having slipped off to the kitchen), Bell brought over the new nurse and said, so loud everybody heard,

"Roger, you've met Miss Archer—"

"Lydia," she corrected, smiling.

"—but I just realized tonight as we were talking that her father is the Rev. Henry Archer, Rector of St. James, and her grandfather on her mother's side was Bishop Sommers. I knew you'd be interested."

"Indeed," I said.

"Since Roger's father, as you doubtless know, was one of the great missionary-doctors on the coast and a friend, a great friend, of your grandfather."

"It is a tight little island, isn't it?" she said, and managed to get off her innuendo with such a zip-ah-dee-doo-dah smile that old Bell never noticed a thing.

"I know you two have lots to talk about," he said, "so I'll leave you to it. I just wanted to make sure you knew Miss Archer, Roger."

"My pedigree, you mean," she smiled sweetly, and he smiled weakly back and then was off, presumably to keep the party moving.

We stood there a moment, not exactly ill at ease but not eager either, parrying. I noticed she had brought a date—Danny.

"Well, Doctor, if you're half as disinterested in your lineage as I am in mine, we can dispense with that topic."

"Fine," I said.

"And launch into the present. Why we're here, for instance. Why are you?"

"Well," I stumbled, "I'm not sure, really; no, not anymore. But then, I'm not accustomed to being asked."

"I'll tell you why I'm here," she said. "To right some of the wrongs perpetrated by our great and illustrious forebears, both yours and mine, Doctor," emphasizing with stacatto precision the words *right* and *wrong* and *doctor*.

"She's bucking for a fight," I thought, "and me ten years tired." If I had learned one thing in my ten years among the Indians, it was retreat. "That's interesting," was all I said.

She glared back, and the violent red hair seemed suddenly lacklustre compared to the glitter in her eyes. "There's a devil in the kitchen, Doctor, and an angel in your bed. Perhaps I'm keeping you from one, or both. Another time?" And stalked off so abruptly I hadn't time to color.

She was like that. Little wonder, then, I saw it coming. When the nurses and the nurses' aids elected her as matron, it seemed new parts were being cast in an old feud. I didn't really know too much about the first one, and I'll wager she knew even less: how my father came as missionary-doctor to the village and built it up, both church and hospital, and started a small school, a village co-op, a sawmill, and a salmon cannery, and had the village nearly on its feet—all this before the Government came in—when the church which sponsored him saw fit, largely due to his success, to make a separate diocese of its Indian missions on the coast and sent a Bishop from England to Nanootkish.

Now this Bishop Sommers, her grandfather, was high-church, my father low-church, and a lot of petty rivalry ensued: the Bishop calling in gunboats to settle their squabbles, and jailing several of the natives, filing false charges against some, and actually striking one or two because they'd remained loyal to father. Admittedly I'm biased, but the upshot of it was that my father was defrocked after twenty years a deacon, but stayed on as head doctor at the hospital he'd started (all the old church-hospitals had by that time switched to government staffing and subsidy), while the Bishop eventually died and, without father behind them, the Indian missions faltered and the diocese died too. Finally the church pulled out entirely and a native Christian church under my father carried on but following his death quarreled over his successor and ended by calling in two missionaries, an Anglican and a Pentecost. It was as though they'd grown accustomed to quarreling. The worst part of it was that the land became an issue, the Bishop when he took over the mission and school-house demanding deed and title transfer from the Province. This coming on the heels of father's dismissal riled the Indians, who called on the Dominion Government to arbitrate. It was the first time any of the Coastal Indians had asked the Government for anything (they have no treaties like Plains Indians). The Government made promises, but got pressure from the Province, and ended by sending in surveyors to stake off a reserve, skirting the two acres in the centre of the village where the school and mission-compound sat! "A fine day for the Church of God," my father often said, "and for the native people of the coast, when Bishops and Blackguards stand together!" It didn't help the villagers' self-confidence, I'll say that much, especially the headmen who against my father's counsel had petitioned the Government for help.

This was about all I knew of the story, only what I'd read and heard at home. We didn't grow up in the village, my brother and I, but downtown with our mother in our summer home. A misnomer, really. Our father would be there some summers, but once the cannery got underway he was kept busy summers too; so we visited the village as a family one month, maybe two months of the year, and never after we reached high-school age. My older brother felt about it like my mother, but I always regretted our short stay. One of my earliest remembrances—I couldn't have been more than three or four—was of father strawbossing the building of the playground. Women and children, bark baskets on their backs, packing gravel in a steady humpbacked line up from the beach where men with shovels worked loading; and as they marched and stooped and loaded, marched and stooped and dumped, moving laterally the whole length of the beach-front, back again, in a rhythmic circle march they chanted Indian and sweated. It was a hot damp dreamy day, the kind of day that flushes faces and squints eyes—the solstice sun so brilliant, the sea so green, the sky so blue, the tide-washed gravel so blue-black and all the atmosphere between charged with expression so intense—so vivid it could only be called lurid. Then a summer shower through a circular rainbow during which the sun refused to hide. I stood beside my father watching, awed—the whole world bathed in greenery, and technicolored sky and sea seemed one that timeless instant—caught up in the chanting march of men, women, and children: a world of order, worship, praise. Some of the older Indians wore brightly colored blankets and walked beside the others, leading singing while looking to my father who would point where the gravel was needed. They clapped hands and sang deep from their throats, a steady marching rhythm with strange words, strange cadences, strange fascinating sounds, dark meanings to a child not yet school age. A world dark, fecund, physical, more vital and intense than the pale hushed hidden-in-my-mother's-skirts world I had known was vividly revealed to me that day. A world I came to think of as my father's world, because standing proudly beside him I saw that it revolved around him: the orders he barked, the names he called, the words of encouragement he gave, the looks of trust and admiration on the men's and women's faces—none of it was lost on me that day. Besides the fact that he seemed more at home there, outdoors working and singing with, as my mother said, "his Indians," than tiptoeing around the mission-house with us. That was the vision I got of him, anyway. And that was the winter we moved downtown.

Life downtown was different, quite different. I lost contact with my father's world, as he had long since lost contact with what my mother interchangeably referred to as "her people," and "civilization." My grandmother lived with us and she was religious, so my mother felt she was fulfilling her wife's vows by living winters in the summer home my father built for her and subjecting her two sons to daily Bible readings because her husband was a minister. She always called him by that title, "minister," not missionary, when people asked about him, and said he was "among the Indians." She was pleased when he took three years off to go through medicine, not for the good it might do Nanootkish, but because she could refer to him as "doctor." We were glad too, though we didn't see him that much, weekends only. One weekend I remember—I was seven or eight then, my brother ten—he brought us home a full-dress Indian outfit, leather chaps and vest and feather headdress. (It was Plains- not Coastal-Indian, but we didn't distinguish.) My brother said he wanted a cowboy suit and thought no more about it; that didn't hurt my father, he'd intended it for me. I wore it once. I knew, the minute I saw it, the kids would razz me. It was *too* nice, too authentic, too expensive for every kid on the block to get one like it; besides, my father was "among the Indians." I knew I'd get catcalls and was embarrassed to wear it; I did, and was ashamed to take it off. Mother put it in mothballs and father never mentioned it, but I felt guilty: I had betrayed my father's world. What else could I do—become the laughingstock of the whole neighborhood? Maybe even, if I didn't go along, get beaten up? Was it so difficult to be an Indian just because cowboys were in vogue among the ten-year-olds that year? Or had it always been, would it always be? I had nightmares and woke up crying for two, three years afterward, long after my father had gone back to the village.

In considering what drew my father back I am, of course, discovering my own motives as well. With me it was never a conscious decision but a compulsion to return home, subterraneous as a tugging in the blood, congenital as a birthmark. Home being in my mother's and the world's eyes a place remote, foreign, forsaken (by God, presumably) and, worst of all, uncomfortable; peopled by an alien tribe, uncouth, arrogant, and ingrates. (Which was worse, that they were "ingrates" or "in hiding," was a toss-up and debated at some length among my

mother's friends: ingrate usually emerging as the term of official
opprobrium, since to adopt "in hiding" would have slurred my
father also, whereas "ingrate" made my father's work of
"civilizing them" part of the golden-goose Civilization they were
in hiding from. It was more inclusive.) Particularly once the
land issue arose and made its way into the papers, and the
Province threatened to secede, and the Dominion intervened,
particularly then did the drawing-room discussions reach new
peaks of rhetoric and cant. I was then in high-school and would
come in on my mother and her friends — old Mrs. Lethbridge
with her hooked nose so askew she looked always on the
verge of saying "Pee-euw!"; and Miss Lily Peter the rancheress
who hired a man to manage her huge stock farm in the Caribou
(one of those they used airplanes instead of horses to ride herd
on); Dr. Jarvis (church, not medical); and Miss Flora Armitage
the retired math teacher. They were all, except the doctor,
members of the Prodeo Club or Ladies' Circle (I forget which;
mother was in both), and Dr. Jarvis was head minister of the
church downtown. "It's a shame," he would be saying, ". . .
a crying shame we have to martyr a good man like Sylvester."

"In this day and age." (Old Mrs. Lethbridge.)

"Precisely."

"You would think, wouldn't you, Doctor, that the Church
wouldn't air its problems to the Government?" (Miss Lily
Peter.)

"I would indeed. Better to suffer wrong, Paul said."

"You forget, Lily, it was the Indians called in the Government." (Miss Armitage. She and my mother always stood
together in these talks.)

"Against Sylvester's better judgement." (My mother.)

"Yes, but the Bishop called in warships first—imagine,
warships!" (Miss Lily Peter) "—to frighten a few Indians. What
if I said to my man, Slim, strafe all mavericks—what kind of
shepherding is that?"

"Worldly, Miss Peter, worldly, but Bishop Sommers is a worldly man."

"They're doing it in Russia." (Old Mrs. Lethbridge.)

"He's English." (Miss Armitage.)

"And the world, ladies, the world is leaving us behind."

"Well, I think Sylvester" (my mother fidgeted with the bridgehand she held) "—up there, with that tribe; a doctor *and* a minister—" (she glanced at Dr. Jarvis) "I think he's hiding his light under a bushel."

"Precisely."

"We need men like him down here." (Old Mrs. Lethbridge nodded vigorously and tapped one finger on the table.) "Pioneers."

"The rich need help more than the Indians." (Miss Lily Peter.) "I've always said."

All nodded.

"Well," (Miss Armitage) "maybe now the Government's stepped in, he'll come downtown."

"This city" (Jarvis wet his lips, weighing his words), "this province even, ladies, is I fear just too provincial for a man as gifted as Sylvester Sharp."

Doctor Jarvis, B.A., B.D., D.D., needn't have worried. It never crossed my father's mind to take a church downtown. He had almost a grudge against the city: not Vancouver in particular, but cities in general. And he had the fixed idea that farm-life, in church terms "a rural charge," was a compromise.

"Mere vacillation and a failed attempt to enjoy both the blessings of Nature and the benefits of Civilization, without embracing either one. Man has been on this earth a million years," he wrote me in my freshman year of medicine, "though what is that compared with dinosaurs? and farming with its parasitic city-growth only five thousand years, yet 'Behold what desolations he maketh in the earth!' " His favorite prophet was an Indian who, after father had been defrocked, he slipped into the Native Christian canon: "in place of St. Stephen who was nuts," he laughed, "or St. Abelard." ("On second thought," he said the next day, "we'll keep Abelard."

"Why?" I asked. "Wasn't Abelard as nutty as St. Stephen, and more learned?"

"We'll keep him," he said, "not for his interminable learning, that's for sure; but because he had the flair to do on the high altar, sober, what the drunken priests were doing in the dark!") This Indian Smohalla who was my father's favorite prophet was the hunchbacked Dreamer who worshipped Mother-Earth and thundered at the white man:

> My young men shall never work. Men who work cannot dream, and wisdom comes to us in dreams.
> You ask me to plow the ground! Shall I take a knife and tear my mother's bosom?
> You ask me to dig for stone! Shall I dig under her skin for her bones?
> You ask me to cut grass and make hay and sell it, and be rich like white men. But how dare I cut off my mother's hair?
> It is a bad law and my people cannot obey it.

A pacifist, preaching this doctrine of passive resistance, Smohalla was credited with the Nez Perce war, the Bannock war, the Modoc war, the Yakima war, and possibly the Sioux Uprising too. Apparently he fought, with words alone, the North Pacific Railway, the Indian Homestead Act, and the U.S. Cavalry. He lost. My father thought him greater than Isaiah. I asked Doctor Jarvis once what he thought about Smohalla.

"Smo-who?" he said.

"Smohalla. The Indian prophet. Nez Perce," I said.

"Nez-what?"

"Pierced nose," I translated, "the pierced-nose tribe."

"Oh, yes," he said, "some of them do that, it's a custom among them, I understand. Who knows, maybe our own people did the same in olden days? We mustn't judge, my boy."

It took a while, but gradually I grew convinced that Dr. Jarvis and the Church, my mother and the world, *her* world, understood my father just as little as they did Smohalla. The only difference was they *thought* they knew my father—he existed—whereas Smohalla and the nameless others never warranted that much, they never were.

The year I finished medical school my father died. My mother insisted on a downtown funeral ("he had friends here, too, you know"); and since my father had specifically requested he be buried on Grave Island, the body was shipped downtown and then back. I had to intern in the city so the village had a two year interim *sans* Sharps.

By the time I arrived at Nanootkish hospital the quarrel over Dad's successor in the church had been settled, and the villagers were busy playing off the two new missionaries. I made damned sure not to get involved. And that occasioned first the comment I would hear time out of mind the next ten years: "Gee-ee, you shure are different than your father, Doctor Sharp!" "Ye-es, your old man was an altogether different man!"

I mention this because I'd always thought we were alike; at least, I agreed with his ideas. But from the time I arrived things started changing in the village—drastically, beyond recall —and it wasn't my presence but his absence, I know now, not what I didn't do but what he'd done. As though singlehandedly my father by sheer will and primal fiat had shored up the very island against sinking, and now overnight the sea upsurged! The people drifting dreamlike down a million or more years now suddenly awoke to a nightmare, shrieking beyond sound that single shrill inhuman shriek, uncertain if the sea were real, unreal, food-garden or asphyxiating flood. Certain only of one thing: that around them where once wilderness was queen now stood the city of the world—inescapable, unpredictable, encircling and upsurging like the flood-tide sea, like drowning. This overnight. And me the doctor, headman, chief!

The suicides began my first year here, with Sady. Needing no occasion, no priming like Mona, only the rebuff, the shrinking back, she stood in my door drenched, mumbling so matter-of-factly, "I've come now, finally. I'm here now." Then, "You don't even know what for, do you? You're different, I can see that. But I've come, I'm here now." Then, when something in her eyes, the hardness, the inscrutible Indianness, kept me from inviting her in even, saying it again, hard and flat, "I'm here now. You're the white man, you're the headman here now. You can have me." And while I stood uncertain and afraid to ask her in, imperceptibly shrinking, sinking inside, thinking, what would *he* do now? what *would* he do? she said without emphasis, almost to herself: "You're not the man. I see that now. They're right," and turned and walked away not briskly, not defiantly but not slouched either, through the driving rain along the boardwalk home . . . and slashed her wrists. This after she had taken the stink-eggs.

I never connected old Chief Blackstock's funeral with the Bishop's coming until, walking down the boardwalk with Lydia on a hospital call, we passed his tombstone (it was in the front yard of his old deserted house, the custom for a person lost at sea).

"Uriah the Hittite," she said, "lost at sea."

"What?"

"Uriah the Hittite," she said, "lost at sea somewhere near Grave Island. His body was not recovered."

"What do you mean, 'Uriah the Hittite'?" I looked at the stone just to make sure I hadn't missed something. "You wear contacts?"

"Wasn't your father's name David?"

"His middle name. Why?" I asked.

"No, *who*? You stutter by any chance? The question now is: Who was Bathsheba?" And she started walking, brisk, straight shoulders set, driving her heels into the boardwalk, that abominable orange hair banging out of its coiled bun.

II

Nora, who had kept house for my father, was now dead, and Chief Jesse Blackstock lost at sea. Their daughter Sady had committed suicide, triggering a decade and half of suttees to some strange god who with Lydia's arrival had changed gender, but not genus, and whose list of sacrificial victims, now young men instead of women, soon would number Sady's son.

Who this Priapus turned Kali was, this demigod who'd driven to despair two generations and was now in a new avatar commencing on a third, had become an urgent question to me since so far as any human agent was involved, my father was the chief suspect. Not directly, but obliquely; and not the only, but the chief suspect—simply because he more than any other person had, for good or ill, had an amazing impact on the village.

Yet behind him, I consoled myself, there loomed the more impersonal masqued power "Civilization": whose tool he was intended as, whose agent he was not, whose actual agent he did battle with. And was it not entirely possible, I asked myself, that this usurper Bishop, grandfather of the very Lydia who accused my father, was himself the arch-antagonist? The true false-priest who for himself spied out and consecrated, with firewater or trinkets from his co-op, the lusty daughters of Peacemaker, and for his granddaughter their sons? Was is not possible? I asked myself. All this accomplished without physical contact since physical contact they understood, had suffered, could withstand; no, somehow more subtly seducing them, inserting (perhaps even with a touch of humor, a wry smile) the debilitating thought, the sly suggestion, the mind-germ—first-cousin to the sperm, but subtler—insinuating (this over a period of years) that they the beneficiaries of gifts were "Indian," thus inferior; entrapped within the skin (dirty) which marked them thus, thus damned; encircled by the mind (superior) which thought them thus, thus doomed (to wage-labor and dependent status); dependent on the hand (beneficent) which fed them candies, cut-rate groceries, ribbons, beads, therefore indebted. Spirit-rape—a highly civilized technique for killing at a distance.

Possible? I asked. I wasn't sure. But surely some first-cause must lurk somewhere in the background, in some actual point of contact or, if non-contact, some discernible moment of mind-rape. And obviously I hadn't plumbed it yet, hadn't dredged it, tumorous and slimy from the bottom of the sewer, hadn't analyzed it yet by light of day. It was, if you will, a medical problem with a metaphysical solution—unless I could identify the germ. And in the forty-two or forty-three suicides I'd witnessed in a decade (this in a population of a thousand), not all of them entered officially as such, but forty-three bodies I'd prepared whose cause of death I'd entered marginalia about in a black ledger, *something* more insidious than whiskey was the cause.

I realized this more acutely than ever when, sitting down to enter Danny's name, as two weeks later I would enter Dean's, I thumbed numbly, nauseously through the "Deaths" ledger, scanning at random one full page:

SURNAME	CHRISTIAN-NAME	SEX	AGE	DATE OF DEATH	CAUSE OF DEATH	DR.
Huckaby	Alice Mae	F	25	1/7/61	1st degree burns	R.S.
Huckaby	Lila	F	2	"	(apparently the	"

Huckaby	Henry	M	4	"	mother, while drunk, tied the children in bed and set fire to the house.)	R.S.
Greene	Silas G.	M	27	2/4/61	asphyxiated while drunk (plastic bag)	R.S.
Blackstock	Gideon	M	47	3/7/61	TB	R.S.
Angel	Tilly	F	3	6/15/61	asphyxiated	R.S.
Angel	Eugene Rex	M	4	"	" (father fell across children while drunk and smothered them.)	"
Fisher	Gale Harvey	M	29	7/4/61	drowned while drunk	R.S.
Snow	Hannah Louise	F	24	7/19/61	suicide (wrists cut)	R.S.
Franklin	Levi	M	56	8/27/61	carcinoma of thyroid gland	R.S.
Woodfall	Elmer	M	38	9/3/61	TB	R.S.
Newberry	Forrest	M	6	9/17/61	drowned (parents drunk)	R.S.
Snow	Mattie	F	1	10/2/61	possible pneumonia (actually the father fell across the child while drunk and smothered her.)	R.S.
Weaver	Nicey	F	22	10/9/61	suicide (wrists cut)	R.S.
Blackwater	Susan	F	116	10/23/61	old age	R.S.
Hunter	Moses F.	M	32	10/25/61	choked on a pork chop bone while drunk	R.S.

It read like a journal of the plague-year—with nine more like it! What a relief to run across an entry now and then as natural and straightforward as TB!

We, the Wilderness

I entered Danny's name, sex, age (26), death date, then wrote "suicide (mental depression)," transcribing in a cold dead hand the mental cipher which meant nothing, the bland footnote which not only did not comprehend but did not even try to comprehend the text it epitaphed . . . the caged fury and last minute's vacillation of the mind, the instant's hesitation of the hand, the finger touching, toying as a child might, then squeezing and the shocked surprise of brains powder-burnt and blasted, splattered on the walls and ceiling of a basement room piled with old boxes, crates—the detritus of days spent captive and entrapped within a wilderness roamed free by animals and white men, a wilderness denied him, Danny (a wilderness denied Dean, too, who less than a week later would pump number-four shot in his stomach, two barrelfuls, after the old twelve-gauge had misfired inside his mouth), though it was his father's and his grandfather's, his ancestor's domain. . . . "Suicide (mental depression)."

No, I hadn't comprehended Danny's death, I wasn't ready to comprehend Dean's—single voices in a chorus forty strong of dead men and women I had dressed and buried, buried and blessed, who together swore a single shrill inhuman curse I had tried not to hear, had stopped my ears against because I hadn't wanted to hear it. Now I did. After Danny's death, before Dean lay dying, I had sworn I would disturb the dead, ransack old records, pillage graves—do anything, so that the carcinomatous mushroom at the bottom of the tomb, the tumor slick and clinging to an old apocryphal curse ("Die," it whispered, and they did) got rooted up. Even if my father was involved, or Jesse Blackstock—whomever—God Himself . . . *Because if I have to stitch another face like Danny's, if I have to.* . . . I decided I needed a trip downtown after Danny's death. First though I would see what old Willie knew about first causes and curses.

Since Granny Blackwater's death (age 116), Willie was

the oldest in the village. Both his and old Gideon Stone's birth-dates were a matter of conjecture, but both had been drawing old-age pensions since the legislation came into existence, and Willie was the better storyteller: he knew English. I knew he had been married to Nora at one time—he her third or fourth, she his seventh—and that he'd been close to my father. Also, he kept a room at the hospital, ostensibly to have his legs dressed daily, but really because he liked being waited on by the young nurses. He'd recently answered a magazine ad whereby a man in Canada could order an Australian bride on a ninety-day trial basis (the marriage within ninety days of arrival, or fare back to Australia guaranteed). He'd sent off one thousand dollars with, I later learned, my picture. The nurse who'd given him the magazine *Down Under* was an Aussie and he'd figured, first, that all Australians looked like her and, second, that it was a recent issue. It wasn't and they didn't but nobody told him different and I found him sitting at the window, both legs propped, gazing out across the water at Grave Island and beyond to distant aphrodisiacal islands where languid women lacked for men.

"Any word on that ad yet, Willie?" I asked, taking a seat beside him at the window.

"Not yet," he said and laughed good-naturedly. "See that snow?" He pointed to where the Straits described a scukumchuk between Grave Island and the mainland glacial range. "She's workin' her way down the mountain now, deer comin' down for matin', good huntin'."

"I hear Sam and Laramie came back with fourteen *mo-witch*, mostly bucks," I said.

He started laughing, first a gentle chuckle then a rotund Santa Claus-type laugh, big belly shaking and the tears starting to roll. It looked like he would never stop. "Your . . . father. . . ." he got out, "your father . . . he talked Indian . . . words too.

And *he* couldn't . . ." (that set him off again) "say them any . . . *bet*-ter!" He went on laughing, whether at my father or at me, or just at life, or at Grave Island, or the prospect of him getting a new bride, or what, I didn't know. Old Indians, I thought, they're all like that: cheerful, childlike. Granny Susan was like that, and old Gideon, Samson, Angus—as though all the hard times are behind them and they've got only good times coming.

"Maybe," he said, breathless from laughing, "maybe when the snow . . . gets to Australia . . . ol' Willie's greenbacks will look good to that . . . young *mowitch!*" and he took a sniff of snuff in each nostril and cleared his throat.

"Willie," I said, "you were good friends with my father?"

"Very good," he said, serious, sincere, as though I'd broached a serious subject. "Your father and ol' Willie were good friends, why, I didn't object when my late wife kept house for him—she lived in, too! Your father needed a wooman around the house. Nothin' meant against your mother, o' course."

"No," I said. "That was Nora, wasn't it?"

"Nora, yes, may God rest her soul. She's buried on Grave Island there, a good wooman. She had—let me see now" (he counted on gnarled fingers, slowly) "—fourteen, fifteen children! Four of 'em mine."

"Willie," I said.

"Yes?"

"Tell me about Nora. And my father. And Chief Jesse Blackstock. And the Bishop. Tell me about all of them, you know their story."

He looked at me as if to say, Which story? Which one of the many hundreds are you after, do you want? Not why, not for an instant, merely which. Gazing quizzically, not at me but through me, rummaging, rifling the archives of his mind, then blinking—you could almost see the flash, the hidden agenda in the forgotten ledger filed forty, fifty years ago, found now—

blinking like a wise old owl as darkness settles and he opens wide his eyes and starts to see, perceive, discern the indiscernible and imperceptible patternings of both the quick and dead he looks both back and down on afterdark. He sees their story, and seeing he tells it, and telling he relives it, and they live: both quick and dead.

"I guess somebody tol' you I ran into Jesse Blackstock," he said. "Yes, somebody had to tell you that, I guess. Might's well be me. Well, Jesse Blackstock was chief's son. You seen his gravestone outside Nora's house?"

I nodded. "Lost at sea," I said with confidence.

"That's what it says." He closed his eyes and intoned as if reading: " 'Jesse Stone Blackstock, son of Stone Blackstock, grandson of Chief Black Stone. 1897–1942. Lost at sea somewhere near Grave Island. His body was not recovered'—it says that. Well, I'm gonna tell you somethin'," he leaned over close and put both hands on my knees. "Chief Jesse Blackstock is alive. I seen him! You remember when I come downtown to see your father a year or so before he passed away? You must have been in medicine school then."

"I think so," I said.

"Well, I come to tell your father I'd seen him, Jesse Blackstock. I'd gone down to have that gallstone operation and was waitin' for a plane back. Weather's bad, so I go in this café in Chinatown a lot of our people used to use. I was sittin' kinda sidewise to the counter when this Indian come in, tall fella with a red-headed white wooman, and I thought he looked familiar but I says to myself, no, that operation's weakened your mind too and went on eatin' till they drew alongside and I stole a sidewise glance and—sure enough! I caught that fella starin'. Which one of us looked down first I can't say, we both looked down so fast, me shovin' in my food so fast I started coughin'. I was scared, I tell you, but I think he was scareder.

He wanted to come over, seen him whisper and that wooman look 'round once when they get to the cashier, but that white wooman she just takes him by the sleeve and keeps on goin'—they never even touched their food!—and by the time I got outside they were across the street and gettin' into a new pick-up truck piled high in back with cabbages and carrots so fresh-picked there was still dirt on, pullin' away.

"Well, I went to tell your father right away and he said, 'Willie, you did right comin' here,' but I could tell he didn't believe me. He asked if I had actu'ly talked to Jesse and I said no, and he asked me then what color his hair was. Why, black, I said, and then it struck me that when he was lost at sea his hair was white—not old age, mind you, but a kinda freak of nature—so your father got *me* wonderin' if I'd seen right. I wasn't sure until I got back to the village and it turned out that I wasn't the first one because Letty was just back from Essendale (the first time, when they sent her down to have that baby) and she said—nobody believed her—that every Monday morning for two years she'd watched 'the Chief' (she called him that still) drive up with a truck of cabbages or carrots or potatoes and unload them at the kitchen door. The inmates weren't permitted to help him, she said, but she'd watched him every Monday through the bars and after she'd had her baby and was workin' in the kitchen she waited by the door one Monday mornin' and said 'Jesse' and he stopped and looked at her so funny, she said, just like she'd stuck a knife in him.

"Then, one day (this accordin' to Letty who nobody believed because before she left she spent most everyday out berrypickin' or bark-strippin' by herself and had those fits, and after she come back she'd got religion and started talkin' to ravens and seein' ghosts and hearin' Jesus), one day Jesse Blackstock spoke to her: 'Letty,' he said, and she said 'Yes?' like it was natural to have Chief Jesse Blackstock speak to her,

man or ghost, dead or alive, as natural as hearin' ravens, 'Yes?'
she said, and he said, 'You know who I am?' 'You're Jesse
Blackstock,' she said, 'Chief of all us Indian people, but where
you get these cabbages and carrots and potatoes with the dirt
still on, I'll never know.' 'I'll tell you,' he said. 'No,' she said,
'I don't want to know. 'Cause whoever heard of an Indian
Chief haulin' cabbages and carrots and potatoes in a pick-up
truck for crazy people? Whoever? Wherever you get them and
that truck you get them in I'll never know, 'cause I don't want
to know.' And Jesse Blackstock, he just stood there in the
kitchen doorway of that crazyhouse, starin'; and Letty was
afraid, she said, that he might hit her, but he didn't; then she
was afraid that he might cry, but he didn't do that either: just
left the cabbages and carrots and potatoes in the door and
she started puttin' them away, and he was gone. 'But it wasn't
Jesse Blackstock anyway,' she said, 'it was Raven'—and maybe
that's why no one believed her—'it was Jesse Blackstock's head,
but Raven's hair.'

"Well, when I heard that, and that people around here
was teasing her for claimin' to see Jesus (*Hemas* in our language means 'Chief,' it means 'Lord' too), I knew it wasn't any
ghost I seen downtown, but Jesse Blackstock. Changed maybe
—he had black hair now, and a white wife, and a new pick-up
truck, and maybe a cabbage-and-potato patch somewhere–but
it was Jesse Blackstock, his youth renewed like Raven's maybe,
but still an Indian, and since we haven't really had a chief since
him, still Chief. I got to thinkin' and rememberin' and wonderin'.
What happened? What made him take off like he did? 'Cause
he was the first one to ever leave this village, to leave and not
come back and never hope to. And him Chief! Oh, ol' Joe Gladstone got drunk in Vancouver once, and the war was on, the
first war, and when he sobered up it turned out he'd been
volunteered and got shipped out all the way to Halifax, by train,
and then by truck, and when they tried to load him on a boat

he fell off the pier in Halifax and drowned; but he got shipped back home for burial and Minnie's got the star yet, and the badges. So I got to thinkin' back, what really happened? What gets into a man to make him do a thing like that? And Nora, his wife then, with seven kids.

"I got to thinkin' and rememberin' and it come to me that Nora when he left was with her eighth, the still-born one they buried the same day they gave up dredgin'. Because even then they couldn't quite believe that Chief Jesse was lost—drowned maybe, but the body would turn up, would float, so they kept dredgin'—Nora waitin' on the dock until she had that still-birth and the spirit seemed to leave her, then they gave up. They had found his skiff, you see, beside his boat the *Sady D.*, but it was loose and driftin' upside-down and underneath the skiff they found his cap. That was enough, or would have been except for Nora. She it was, I think, boarded his boat first and discovered that the suitcase with his downtown clothes was missing; but she didn't mention it to anybody then, just kept them dredgin' a full week or ten days for the body, till her time come. Then she went in and your father delivered the still-birth and the spirit seemed to leave her for a time—she almost died she tol' me later—and your father walked right out of the hospital to the church and conducted the two funerals that day. It took all day, too, because Jesse was chief's son and the baby that was still-born was a boy, their first son. They'd had seven daughters to that time and that alone, I guess, would be enough to get a man down. Anyway, most people blamed the still-birth on the drownin' (Nora herself tol' me that the baby was kickin' right up to the last week or ten days) so it seemed the thing to do to have both funerals and, anyway, there would of been no body otherwise.

"They buried him, it, in the plastic bag inside the man-sized coffin, and the band played: one of the last times I can remember since ol' Gideon the bandleader had his teeth pulled that same year, and most of us already had false teeth. So there was somethin' your father started that just fell apart when Jesse Blackstock left. The spirit seemed to leave us then, I don't know why."

"You lost your lip," I offered.

"We lost our head," Willie said simply. "You see this hat?" He pulled out of the paper bag in which he kept his clothes an old conductor-type blue hat with frayed gold braid, discolored where the sweat-band had worn thin. Above the brim three tarnished metal letters hung from pins. "This hat," he said, wiping the brass letters on his sleeve, not vigorously in any vain attempt to shine them, but with delicacy, care, as though caressing a touchstone, "this hat was the headdress your father gave us, these letters, N., C., B.,"—he pronounced the letters slowly, deliberately, as though cherishing each one—"stood for the 'Nanootkish Concert Band.' The N.C. also stood for 'Native Christian.' And 'Band' means not only brass band, but the clan, the tribe we revived under your father. When *he* left. . . ." Willie lapsed into long silence, pondering the faded hat with a bemused, bewildered, almost childlike expression, as though he held the emblem of all fortitude and hope, the panache which blazoned forth in tarnished letter and gold braid a cryptic key he could no longer decipher, no longer *grasp*, ". . . he left," he concluded, staring at the hat.

"You mean my father, when *he* left?"

"*Hemas*," he said, as though avoiding the question; then: "Your father, Jesse Blackstock—*Hemas*, when he left."

"But that was only '42. Dad didn't leave till '52. The Bishop had yet to arrive, and. . . ."

"Your father stayed on quite a while, it's true, but the spirit seemed to leave him after that," he said simply.

"Even before the Bishop came?" Then, when he continued either to brood or to consider the matter self-evident and therefore closed, I added: "It's kind of important to me, Willie."

"Around then," he said vaguely. "But it wasn't the Bishop," he started suddenly, as though the wise old owl had spotted prey, "it wasn't the Bishop with his warships and surveyors and tin star—that's what we called the jail he built on Mission Point, his tin star—it wasn't him. Your father had been headman in this village twenty years or more; he could have raised his black flag on that Bishop."

"His black flag?"

"The black flag he had hoisted whenever anyone he didn't like come to the village. Mostly Indians from other tribes who wouldn't come to church, but some rum-runners too—Swedes, Russians, Bostonmen—and Indian or white they left right quick!"

"I see," I said. It was something I had never heard about my father.

"We tried to tell him when that Bishop first arrived, hoist the black flag, we said. But he said no; a Bishop is or ought to be a man of God, he said, we won't black-flag him. Even after he had brought those people in (your father was away then) to say your father wasn't pastor anymore, and even after he took over the church-building and the mission-school and manse, and started up a second co-op store—cut-rate, because he used church funds—even then your father said no, wait, he said." Willie shook his head sadly. "The spirit left him long before that Bishop come. It left around the time Chief Jesse did. Chief Jesse, your father, the Spirit—all left together, pretty near. And when the *Spirit* left, the village just went down— band didn't play, chief didn't lead, church started fightin' over land. It was like your father was in mournin' for the chief, and the village was in mournin' for 'em both."

"My father and Jesse Blackstock were that close?" I asked, surprised.

"Ever since that time they stood together in the hall, the old men on one side and the young men on the other, and the old men said in our language they didn't want that game, the one you throw a round ball through a hoop—"

"Basketball, you mean."

"That's it, and the young men said they did and then ol' Chief Black Stone—that was Jesse's grandfather—got up and told how in the old days when somebody was about to die or a Haida war-canoe was sighted, trouble comin', they threw a round thing through a hoop high up in the longhouse and whenever it went in it meant death comin'—he told them that and Jesse Blackstock, he was just a young guy then, got up and said they'd have it anyway and it was tense, the ol' Chief glarin' down on him and Jesse, who would one day be the chief and was supposed to keep the old ways, talkin' back and not even talkin' in our language. It was tense and the ol' Chief wouldof won and that wouldof meant the end of Jesse Blackstock in the men's eyes if your father hadn't lifted up (you know the way it says in the Good Book Moses lifted up his hands, and when he lifted up his hands they victoried, and when his hands fell they was beaten back?), well, your father lifted up his hands for Jesse Blackstock on that day and the ol' Chief, the ol' men, they were beaten back and we got basketball that day and two new headmen, young guys too. That's why the people here blame basketball."

"Blame . . .?"

"Young Danny, he was team captain, you know. But not him only, all those young woomans too, startin' awhile back with Nora's girl, Sady. The ol' folks blame 'em all on that new game."

I could see me writing under "cause of death," entry after entry and *ibid.* after *ibid.*: "basketball; aboriginal attitude toward, bewitched by," and the Medical Society sending a psychiatrist to Nanootkish to examine me. Still, it was an improvement over "mental depression."

"What about you, Willie, what do you think?"

"Me?" he said, "I believe. . . ." but just then the nurse came in—Lydia, yes—plumping a hospital luncheon tray through the door like it was a gift marked personal. Willie's eyes lit up, then glazed again when he spied the tiny package of saltines (saltless), the smallish glass of milk (skim), and a shallow side-bowl of tomato soup (diluted).

"Sweets for the sweet," Lydia sang cheerily, handing him a saccharine tablet for his tea which would come later. He mechanically began unwrapping his saltines.

"Oh, by the way, Doctor," she sang out in an off-hand, over-the-shoulder lilt while straightening the bed, "the Mormons apparently be-*lieve*—" giving the spread a tug "—that the lost tribe of Israel were Indians, American Indians. Doubtless you've heard?"

"Yes," I said.

"But the British Israelites—you know, the bores that beat the Boers—figure they're it."

"Well, so?"

"Well, I was just wondering, Doc-*tor*—" she beat old Willie's pillow till I winced "—if Nora's was the fatal dower, whose might be the new red power? Who do you think? Hmmm?"

"Well, I really. . . ." I began.

"Or, to put it another way, if Jesse was the new Jew's boy, who might be the golden Goy? Any hunches? I've been glancing through the *Book of Mormon* lately. What a gas! You know what I think?"

"I never really. . . ."

"That Uriah the Hittite is alive and well, and hiding in Vancouver, and likes red-heads!" Then, wheeling suddenly and bringing all that concentrated *savoir-faire* and trenchant wit to bear on Willie munching his cracker: "Remember, now, no seconds. Got to slim you down for when *she* comes!" She pointed, and Willie's ruminative gaze followed her finger out the window, remembering probably the food burned on Grave Island before and after every funeral. And while he sat thus rapt she took his tray, one saltine which he wasn't quick enough to snatch exiting with her. Willie wiped his mouth, sighed, and ponderously lowered one leg from the chair.

"Willie," I said. He blinked drowsily. "Did the Bishop have a wife?"

He lowered his other leg. "Jus' like your own mother," he said, "lived downtown. 'Cept she was a red-head, Simon says—he met her once. Nice-lookin' wooman too, Simon says."

"I see. Willie, just one thing more."

He blinked, a little blear-eyed now; a drowsy old owl, naptime.

"That Aussie girl you sent off for, did you order a brunette or a blonde?"

He laughed and heaved up from the chair. "Neither. I ordered me a red-head! All us Indian people likes red-heads—always been that way. That's why those Hudson's Bay men, Scots and Irish, done so well; if they'd sent Swedes they'd never got a fur!"

"Sweet dreams, Willie, and may you live to be a hundred!"

"A hundred and twenty," he corrected me, and climbed in bed.

I went back to my office, remembering to stop by the hospital kitchen and change Willie's caloric intake to "normal." Having locked the office door, I pulled out of a seldom used file cabinet an old black ledger in my father's hand. I didn't know if he'd kept hospital records separate from church, and whether maybe the church records might contain more detail; if so I was up a *cul-de-sac*, but even if they did, I felt sure the information I wanted wouldn't have been recorded. In any event, I wasn't about to ask Rector Bell to show me the church records. So I dug, for what I wasn't sure, and discovered, to what end I couldn't tell, this entry dated September 7, 1942:

"*Born* a son, to Nora Blackstock—stillbirth—LBM." (No father was recorded and it was initialled, not by my father, but by the nurse on duty, LBM.) On the opposite parallel column:

"*Died* Jesse Blackstock, M., 45—accidental drowning." This last was crossed out and inserted in its place: "cause unknown/ body not recovered—SDS."

I thumbed through the staff register and found in 1943 a letter recommending a Miss Lila Brampton Marsh, R.N., to the matron's post at Coquilitza Indian Residential School. And at that point, as the Afrikanders say, "*Die spoor loop dood*"—the trail ran dead.

I put away the ledgers and the stupid and quixotic quest I'd embarked on, and peered out the window where tomorrow the seaplane from Vancouver would touch down, load up, and spirit me away. But it was prematurely dark outside, rainy as always. The channel separating the village from Grave Island was barely discernible through the rain-splayed glass, an intermediate patch of grey, the dark blob of Grave Island beyond it. For no reason, I switched off the light. The ragged outline of Grave Island grew distinct, the channel flowed. It wasn't far, and without lights the village and Grave Island looked the same. Except for a few twenty-five and forty watt bulbs run off the village generator—the same generator my father had shipped in—Grave Island might have been the village, and the village Grave Island.

Upstairs, Willie would be getting a good supper, his reward for having played my Sancho Panza for a day. That tale about the basketball decision: he knew then, at least he knew now he knew then, and had been playing Sancho Panza all these years to my father. Jesse Blackstock too. Was he the first to realize and to rebel against this Tonto role? And did that first initial realization spread till it affected even the dullest, the most diehard? Even as more recent and more subtle realizations spread like a contagion, a huge wen. Hell, leave that to Tonto! I wasn't the Lone Ranger, for Christ's sake—*salvator mundi* either! I'd get the hell out to the city where at least consciousness was king, even if it was fragile and sonic as struck glass.

The city, I thought, peering out my rain-splayed window at eternal dark and brooding taiga, brooding over a grey ocean, greyer in its other and more ancient pre-creation, older even than this world; while fluttering ephemeral five hundred miles away the city, neon-lit, a million-eyed night insect blinking back at me, beat brief and vain against a million miles a billion years of brooding wilderness. And even it, civilization, that ephemeral insect without heritage or lineage, without descent or future, didn't spring phoenix-like from the same anonymous ash but took root and bole and leaf and bud from the same antediluvian boredom, the same aboriginal *ennui* islanding me. Yes, if it comes to that, I thought, if it should come to that—my chauvinistic crusade for first cause and curse—I'll know this much: not so much that he determined them, as that they determined him; as the island doesn't determine the ocean islanding it.

BOOK TWO

Vina
Hazen
Crow
Kaleb
Letty

Vina

All day we heard the seaplanes piloting the schoolkids out; we could not see them for the mist but heard the planes and knew that they were gone. The men left earlier, their ghost boats disappearing in the fog before daybreak. The few who missed their fish-boats ventured out mid-morning, holding one another up and slipping in the rain, feeling in the chill and wet very much alone. It was a grey day, a dismal Sunday finishing a week of Sundays. A feeling of endings without beginnings, of being left alone again, of winter coming—after a short and chilly rainy summer, a poor season—a rainy and grey day. Even though there was and would be preparation for the winter, putting up fish, pulling down blankets, still a sense of waiting without hope, without dread even, of having at last by-passed what we so long dreaded, like the ocean-liners that passed by the village while it slept, their passage punctuated by fog-horns. Some endings were final, eternal as Grave Island; others only seasonal, recurrent. But endings, whether lasting or loose-ends we felt all day: hearing but not seeing the kids leaving, and the rain and loudtalk on the boardwalk, and the missing boats that let us know our men were fishing. A bleak day signaling the end of a bleak season, the beginning of an even bleaker one.

I am watching out my store-front window, flanked by dry goods, glassed candy, and cans—a strip of fishnet decorates each shelf, a locked gate guards the counter—watching Crow, Berriman, and Barrie (though it could be any three, could be

We, the Wilderness

Raymond, if he were alive, could be Crow, Dan and Danny, Slim and Seaborn with Crow, always Crow): watching them maneuver the boardwalk in delicate swagger from Berriman's to Crow's, always Crow's. Crow pauses periodically to hack, spit, miming, Wait! Watch! with that slurred and spastic flourish, then crouching paratroopered on the boardwalk edge he jumps, falls rather, in the slush. Now Berriman, now Barrie follow suit; advancing now the three of them through brittle berrybush and knee-deep slush toward Crow's, intent as little boys at mock-war.

How often standing at this counter during the noon hour, or after school dispensing cans of pop, chips in waxed bags, hard candies from a glass, how many hundred times the brief transaction: children dropping handfuls of wet coppers in my hand, slick hands darting quicker than I can deflect them, fishing under glass, then popping in their mouths jawbreakers, licorice, spice balls; while I glance up, away from drooling chins and decayed teeth and, there, those three again! not always the same three but always Crow, always drunk, maneuvering in delicate imprecision the boardwalk always slick his slow way home. While I peer anxiously—no, not even anxious anymore, just curious—to see who's with him this time: is it Dan? it couldn't be Danny, Raymond's safe now too. Thinking, between the schoolkids and the men outside, the shelves and the counter, always the same thought: that if the men behaved like men the women wouldn't have to. It's because we put up with it. Put up with their sneaking back and forth between house-parties, sneaking to the boats for "stags" and back again, sneaking into bed too drunk to care or if they care too limp to do anything about it. Put up *and* shut up—that's a woman's lot. Some things though you can't shut up, even if you put up with them, some things like bad blood cry out and you can't shut them up. You can't.

Like Raymond. When he was born he was so pretty,

wasn't even swollen, such a pretty baby; but I heard the nurses talking and they'd covered up his feet. I sat up and I said, let me see his feet. They said, he's all right, such a pretty baby, Vinny. Let me see his feet! I said. They looked at one another, then the doctor nodded and the nurse took off the sheet. It was club feet, my pretty baby boy had club feet! I told Dan—he thought Raymond wasn't his—I told him, "It's bad blood between us, Dan."

"Psh," he said, "that old wive's tale, and you're young yet and no wife, no wife to *me*."

Then he started in about his first wife, and Danny, how Danny was a son to him and Nora was a wife, a wife to him.

"And to a lot of others," I said.

And he said, "I admit it. That's what drove me from the bed to the bottle."

And I said, "Raymond's yours."

And he, in that hang-dog way he has: "I accept it. I accept the full responsibility."

So our marriage wasn't what you'd call exactly "happy," but whose is? I had Raymond, then Venita, a five year break, then the twins; I also had the store to keep, Venita helping. He had Danny and his bottle. I didn't mind the two of them around the house until the winter Raymond fell through the pond ice and drowned. Danny it was took him up to where the kids were skating, and it was Danny tried to get him out. He almost drowned himself—it wasn't his fault. No, even after that I didn't mind the two of them, Danny sitting around sullen and Dan drunk, until that summer three, four years ago when Venita got her period. She told me, and I made the mistake of telling Dan. He told his mother.

I had kept Venita home from school thinking she might get embarrassed since we only had the packing paper from the crates. It was noon and I was in the store when they came in— Dan's mother Maggie, and her sister, her oldest daughter, and their friends, eight or nine in all—and found Venita in the kitchen drinking pop and carried her like she was crippled to her bed. They'd stripped her down and put her into bed when I came in and I could see the girl was scared when her grandmother, Fat Maggie, drew this sharp stone out and scratched her just enough to hurt on what we'd always called her "rosebuds," then handed the sharp stone to Janet her sister to string on a necklace and hang around Venita's neck. They started chanting then, producing rattles and Fat Maggie beating time on the bedpost with a blunt stick. Venita started whimpering, scared stiff and goose-pimpled all over when they lifted up the sheet, clinging fearful to the little girl she wasn't anymore, the little girl both son and daughter to me "now a woman" (they were singing), "child no more." The gifts began then: fancy cape and feather head-dress, dancing moccasins, rattle, and spirit-mask. These were her great-grandmother's, old Phereba's, and it was a mark of favor beyond namesake and blood-right that Venita, Vina's daughter, should receive them. I knew that. They didn't have to tell me, not in front of my own daughter, that I was and always would be an outsider; that she wasn't, as of that hour, day—because she was a Blackstock, a chief's granddaughter—not only not a little girl, but no longer Vina's daughter. They said it, and I took it saying nothing, standing pat like a cigar-store Indian (which is what they took me for, I guess, because they hung a blanket on me and put thirty dollars in my hand: the dowry, I suppose, the price of blood). That's why I calculate that day as the beginning, if it wasn't always there, of bad blood between Dan's people and myself. Venita was the first (I won't say Raymond: he was always mine); Venita's was the first blood shed, and Danny's followed. One for one: the village against me, me against the village; Dan's people struck me first, and I struck back.

I never could have done it without Crow. Soon now, within the hour, I will watch him thread his way back down to Berri-

man's, or on to Seaborn's, or maybe to the store for cigarettes
and back again. I will drop what I am doing and look out with
the same instinct that tells old folks rain is coming, scanning
the boardwalk and bushes as they scan the sky, and there'll be
Crow: peeing maybe in the bushes, or weaving between houses,
as constant out my window as rain in a rain forest, and as wel-
come. There'll be Crow, flanked by sidekicks of the moment,
hangers-on (Berriman might last out the afternoon; Barrie's too
young), Crow who for all his drinking is yet man enough to fall
prey to a woman's wiles, yet vain enough never to admit it.
There'll be Crow, bluff, but plenty of bite too, passing on while
others passing out take in one party, maybe two, to his six or
seven nightly. There'll be Crow, not fully conscious but not
oblivious either of the part he played in Danny's suicide.

Dan gets up. He is rummaging around the kitchen. Fat
Maggie who moved in to do the food for the funeral last week
is gone now, the kitchen is a wreck. "Vinny!" he yells at me
through two closed doors, "Laa-*vin*-ee-ah!" I wait. He rummages
a little longer, finds nothing. He's coming now. "Vinny,"—before the door is halfway open—"where's Venita gone to?" I
turn and arch my eyebrows. "Where's Venita?" he repeats,
more civilly.

"Think," I say.

He puzzles. "What's today?" he asks, studying his watch.
"She's not gone, is she?"

"Yes," I say, while he shrinks visibly before me, "she took
the plane this morning. But were you looking for Venita, or for
food?"

Dan blinks, still shrinking backward, shriveling. "Don't
worry," he says, and his voice has that raspy sound.

"He's dry," I think. "He sees me and he suddenly goes
dry and starts to sweat."

"Don't worry about me. I'll be gone a little while. Don't
worry about locking up, I've got a key." And turning, half asleep

still, he trips on the door-stoop. "Damned thing!" he mutters kicking it. "Remind me to fix it tomorrow." And closes the door twice to demonstrate the looseness of the stoop, before he disappears into the house and out the door.

It wasn't difficult. A man like Dan is always ready, even eager, to blame someone, and the person he likes most to blame is Dan. I counted on that, and on Crow's cocksureness: cocksureness that must always crow, bluff, and finagle to appear in the best light. Men are consistent, anyway. And boys, little boys like Danny, feel ashamed if they aren't as bull-headed as men. So, given the three of them, it wasn't hard. Only, Danny had more to him than I'd figured, I admit that, and I'm sorry it turned out the way it did. But I'm not like Dan, I won't accept full blame even for the women since that nurse, the fiesty one who acts like a bitch in heat until, as Crow puts it, "you get her down," got mixed up in it—a hothead, that Lydia, zigzagging like heat lightning through an otherwise all-Indian summer.

It started, I suppose, one day months ago when Crow came in the store—Danny and Hazen were with him—for a case of pop and cigarettes. Just for the hell of it, or maybe because Danny was with him, when I handed him the change he tricked my palm with his finger. "Just for the hell of it," he said, grinning his little boy's grin, and the boys didn't know whether he meant the case of mixer, or life in general, or the bad weather, but they grinned with him while I considered it a second, then said, "You're right, Crow, it would be." And he: "What isn't? Tell me that." And I: "Some things," then added, "maybe." And he: "Maybe. Like this party at my place tonight, it's Milly's birthday. You and ol' Dan are coming, aren't you? Why don't you?" Then Hazen piped in, "What about us, Crow? What about Danny'n me?" And he: "Hell, you boys live there." And I: "Should I bring anything?" And he: "Just bring yourself and — a twinkle in his eyes —ol' Dan."

By time Milly cut the cake Old Dan had passed out, and

since she was a nurses' aid and had to work the midnight shift, she and the white nurses left after cake and coffee. That left fifteen or twenty of us drinking to loud music, with seven or eight more passed out on the kitchen floor or in the bedroom, mostly boys. Danny, though, stayed sober and about eleven-thirty when the nurses left, he left to walk Lydia back to the hospital. A few minutes before midnight the lights gave their warning flicker, then went out. Angie, Crow's eight-year-old, came down in her pyjamas with two kerosene lanterns—her mama told her to, she said—then trundled off to bed again in the attic. Crow placed them on opposite window sills in the big almost bare room (though Milly made good money, Crow had ruined all their furniture through years of drinking), and came round and replenished all our drinks: straight scotch, water if you wanted it, no ice, grinning as he passed me and doing a little dance step— "Jus' for the hell of it!" he announced to everybody—to let me know he was still up to scratch and still itching. "To the hell of it!" I blurted, proposing a new toast, and everybody stood and drank to it. As I said, there were fifteen or twenty of us still, and I wondered how he meant to pull it off. The attic beds were full of children, sleeping supposedly, but running back and forth between their beds and the stairway overlooking the big room. The back master-bedroom was clogged full with coats and passed-out boys sleeping on the coats, while the kitchen, whose hanging hurricane lantern shed light into the big room too, was littered with dead bottles, spent popcans, trays of picked-at food and coffee cups, as well as Dan, Josh, Berriman, and, I think, Myrna, in varying angles and degrees of never-neverness. Exactly what or, better, how and where Crow had in mind, I wasn't sure, but I assumed he knew me well enough to be discreet.

I was wrong—not only about Crow, about myself. Another drink and Hazen went into his false teeth act, Laverne went home, and Freddy Matson started peeing on the floor. He always

does. That's why Milly, and Myrna, Berriman's wife, and Mona
Matson have no rugs now, just linoleum, and those who do have
rugs won't drink with Freddy Matson. It's disgusting, a grown
man like that. While Hazen's little trick is cute or it becomes
him. You see him—always after midnight and lights out—
crawling hands and knees under the furniture (just like that
preacher, they say, when he's lost his glasses), and you try to
plot his course by the giggles; sometimes they fool you though,
giggling in advance—Mona Matson, or Myrna—and you think
he's over there across the room and then you feel his moon-face
thrusting up between your legs and you think, "I won't giggle,
I won't!" but then you have to, you can't help it, 'cause he's
tongued you where it's tender and you picture Hazen Moon
without his teeth where nobody, but nobody! should be, and
you start giggling (and of course at the same time squeezing
him between your thighs like a tree toad catching flies, eyes
blinking and tongue darting till you're giggling so hard you let
go and he's off and up another tree). That's Hazen and he's cute
about it; Freddy Matson though is just disgusting. Loud, and
he gets louder, then he jumps up (on a table if one's handy)
and pulls his thing out and starts aiming it at everybody, turning
in a circle yelling "EEEeeee-" (and as it starts to spout and he
turns faster) "-aaaAAHHH!" Laughing too, that loud, crude laugh
—I don't know how Mona lives with it! Well, Freddy Matson
started spraying from above while Hazen from below searched
for his teeth, and Mona had passed out and Laverne gone home
so there was no one to stop them, and Seaborn—something I
had never seen *him* do before—got down with Hazen on the
floor, so there's two of them now you can't plot by the giggles
because Seaborn I imagine, I don't know—I didn't stay around
to find out— wouldn't be so cute about it and he weighs at least
two hundred and fifty, what with Andy on his back that makes
five hundred.

Anyway, it was then Crow made his move, he stumbled

(it looked like) into my chair and knocked me over, only that was his excuse for catching me and crying, "Jesus! are you hurt?" and carrying me, not to the kitchen though it looked like that was where, but through it and the woodshed past the outhouse to the smokehouse where a little fire was smouldering, and he'd taken off the damper up above the racks of salmon so it wasn't all that smoky and I saw, about the time he pulled my panties down and bra—oh, he undressed me proper, I'll say that—and started nuzzling all over and kissing and caressing my soft spots, I saw a jag of summer lightning zigzag the salmon sky, Indian summer, and I heard just as he slipped it in me, breathing hard now, sultry, someone running and dull thunder drum the sky. I gasped then, shocked, amazed; then I screamed. It was like when I had the twins the first one came out hard and I screamed then, too, straining—more surprised than hurt, because the second one slid out just like a fish.

Call it unnatural or unmanly of him, but I will say this, I will: that was the most sockeyed sensation I have ever had or ever hope to have. I watered quick; and that's something I had never in my life done—who cares how or where?—that's something that it took a man to think of, it took a man to put it in and pull it off. Only, it wasn't quite so smooth 'cause there stood Danny in the smokehouse door, gawking, and Crow jumped up quick, quite self-possessed though (I was glad his pants weren't down) and played a face-card.

"Boys when they get the wrong outhouse should always knock." He bluffed, and took the trick 'cause Danny started fumbling with his zipper, thrown off-guard.

"I just . . ." he stuttered, gaping over at me, ". . . thought I heard. . . ." and Crow tried a trump and blew the game.

"Was it your mother you were wanting," Crow asked him, "or me?"

Danny stared at me, and then at him, then back at me, and you could see he hadn't got it quite, but he was getting it, he'd understudied Crow long enough that it was coming, and he had the general idea. Then he glanced up through the racks of drying fish and I remember thinking to myself, "It's coming, no use my lying here, it's coming," and I gathered myself up—not quick, I couldn't, because my body felt all water still, like when you step from a warm bath to a cold room—I drew up limb by limb and, even in that air, deliciously, and in the time it took me (moving like a stunned fish, fumbling with buttons, bra snaps, hooks-'n-eyes) to get my dress on, he had got it, it had come to him.

He uttered a half-cry and pointed: "She's not!" he cried. "She's not, she's not my mother! And you're . . ." pointing at Crow now.

". . . I'm not your father, no," Crow agreed, then playing a card I didn't think he had and, having, didn't think he'd play: "But who is? Tell me that. Who is?"

And Danny: "I know who."

And Crow: "Do you? You're better off than most then, better off than any Indian."

And Danny stared at him, and then at me, and I knew Crow had played his ace-trump now, and Danny knew (or didn't know) and stood there beaten and perplexed, staring, when Lydia arrived from the hospital and called "Danny," but never got a chance to talk to him because he wheeled, and screaming "Get out! Get out of here!" went running past her nobody knew where.

It was to his great-grandmother Phereba's he went, I later heard. I guess he figured she, if anyone, would know. Which only proves how naïve boys are. Though in this case she did know (most everybody did, must have, if Crow knew); she wouldn't tell him though. So he went next to the one man who should have known, but didn't, the one whose standing and status was in question, Dan himself, to answer for himself and lay to rest all doubt forever and ever.

I could have told him how that meeting would turn out. Old Dan is resting, half-reclining on the couch. Draped with the crazy-quilt Fat Maggie made, his bloodless face and blood-shot eyes blank, pondering for hours the "Certificate of Merit" that he and every other Indian over sixty received simply for breathing and limping through a dance Centennial Year. Dan is resting between drinking bouts when in rushes Danny—breath-less, urgent, poised in mid-flight between the old man hung-over and sweating on the couch and the certificate of merit hanging on the wall. Not waiting like an Indian or a son would wait. I slip into the kitchen and see Old Dan look up dully, bear-like, as though bothered by a gnat or a mosquito, not turning his at-tention to it fully for, whatever the urgence, it will pass on as everything urgent—young blood, lust, vengeance, thirst for truth, for water even—passes on and sleep, deep sleep, blots out all urgency.

". . . if it's true," young Dan is goading, "if what they're saying's true, old man. I want to know!" Not waiting like an Indian would wait, not resembling the old man either, now I see the two together, overhear them from the kitchen.

"I'm tired," the old says; "another time," and rests his aching head and shuts his eyes.

"Fuck you!"

The old man's eyes flick open now. "What's that? What did you say?"

"Right now! I want to know if you're. . . ." Danny begins, falters. "Crow says you're not. . . ."

"What did you say?" Old Dan is rising from the couch.

". . . even my father," he trails off, waiting now.

They stand so: Danny blocking the certificate of merit, Old Dan rising like a bird from off the couch, crazy quilt draped over one arm out-thrust to support him, his face not bloodless now but throbbing, neck and temples, hook-nose and high cheekbones like a bird's.

We, the Wilderness

"Get out!" he roars, swishing the crazy-quilted arm like a great wing: "Get out of my house!"

Then when Danny, braced and hardly breathing even, doesn't move, Old Dan swoops at him like an eagle at a mouse and Danny, bigger than the old man, younger, stronger, throws up both arms as though to ward off beak and blows, uttering a cry, a squeak of terror, and runs out, dodging the uplifted blow that never fell. Old Dan is left, smaller suddenly, more ancient, confronting the certificate of merit. I close the kitchen door and slip quietly into the storeroom at the back.

There was nothing I could do. It was the blood. Blood crying, hurting to be heard. And Danny's none of mine, none of Dan's either. But Old Dan got mixed up in it when he got mixed up with Nora, and Nora got mixed up with God knows who all and how many, Nora was the carrier I say. They say she had TB, I wouldn't know; but I do know that not long after Danny and Old Dan had that run-in, one night late (he had already gone to bed and I had put the twins down and was getting ready for bed myself) Dan called out, "Vinny! Were you in here?" "No," I said, "I wasn't." "Mix me some hot chocolate or something, someone's hooked my mouth and holding me." He couldn't move, he said, for fear his mouth would rip. Just like a fishhook, or someone's finger in his mouth, and pulling his mouth open toward the ear. Just like he was a fish, he said, and had to go with it or rip his mouth. And that was the same night Danny tried to drown himself.

It's a long, narrow way, they say, and three times now when I lay awake at night, my sister, then my brother who was drowned, and lately Raymond come for me. "Come with me," they say, "walk with me." But I only go halfway . . . halfway. My brother—he was drowned, they never found him—said, "It's taken me three days to get here." He was wet too. "There's a big boat waiting for me," he said, "come with me."

But I only went halfway and called out, "Come back, Raymond!" "I have to go now," he said, "it'll soon be daybreak." And it was. That's why I say it's in the blood and blood is thicker than water and if there's bad blood between you, like between Danny and Dan, or Kaleb and young Dean, no sea's deep and no sleep long enough to keep bad blood from coming up, time out of mind, till it's driven every last one to the grave.

Hazen

I hear 'em talking, Carter and them down't the store, they think
it's easy. "Lookit the Indians," they say, "don't have to work.
Just lay around and drink and don't pay tax, I wish *I* could!"
Then steps behind the counter and cheats us. But it's not easy.
One'a the hardest things in the world to do is nothin': nothin'
to do, just lay around all day and come night-time what's there
to do?—nothin' but drink. I'm not like Crow. When Carter laid
me off I wouldn't beg him, not like Crow, an' I never showed
up half as drunk as him!

If it wasn't for the team I'd never've quit: somethin' to
do nights. Even after Danny cut out, and Dean started going
with that nurse and cutting practice, I stuck with it. An' it
happen to me, somethin' happen to me—changed, I changed. I
cut out all my flukes and played it straight. An' it was high-
time, over-time, when a guy like Danny and (I can't believe it
yet) Dean cuts out, I can't believe they're gone—Danny gone
and Dean goin'—I can't believe they're gone an' I'm still here.

'Cause Dean was my left hand. Anytime anybody'd pick
on him I was right there; anybody'd pick on me, he was right
beside me. When Dora Woodfall went to get her baby the team
flipped and twice tails turned up—Hazen, Hazen—Dean went
with me. "Wait up," he said, "wait up, I'll go with you." So
both of us went up to Doctor Sharp and handed him the money
and said, "This's for Dora. We're not sure which of us, but . . .

from the team." And Sharp looked at us a minute, Dean and me, and shook his head and said, "I see. So that's how it is, is it?" And Dean said, "That *is* how it is," and handed him the money and walked out. And Dora got her baby and it wasn't two months later she got big again; but it wasn't Dean or me *that* time, it wasn't the team either, though we sent her a donation for old times' sake.

First time Dean brought me to his place we'd been drinkin'. I hadn't been in Nanootkish since I was a kid, when they sent me off to residential school. I hadn't seen Laverne since then. Laverne was home. So was Dean's father, Kaleb.

"This's Laverne," Dean said, "my big sister." And to Laverne, I still remember: "You know the guy I been tellin' you about—Hazen?—well, this's him." "This's Laverne," he said to me.

I took one look at her, big girl, an' I guess it was the Indian in me: "I'm not afraid," I said, "how 'bout a date?" I said that to her.

I must've been already drunk 'cause Kaleb (he was sittin', pickled, in old man Gideon's chair) heaved up and sortof thrust his arm between us. "You don't do that," he said and I could see how big he was, "this's my daughter."

"I am," I said, "I'm doin' it. This time I am."

And Kaleb he put down his drink and said, "You don't do that, boy, and you don't talk that way either." Then he looked at us, at Dean and me, "You two tough-guys," he said, "I know he'll help you." He looked at me, then Dean.

"He's not helpin' me," I said, "not this time." And quicker'n sight he straight-armed me, *that* hard, an' I got up and sortof fell against Laverne and started kissin' on her, an' Kaleb grabbed me by the scruff and threw me out.

He shouldn't 've done that, 'cause after that Laverne sided with me. She'd never've looked twice at me if Kaleb hadn't stiff-armed me like that, and thrown me out. But why, why didn't he tell me then? He must've known!

Laverne was seein' me, she'd slip out every night and meet me at Crow's place, or their woodshed, or the beachhouse, and then it was too late. It wasn't until after Laverne got pregnant Kaleb told me that my mother had been married to old Gideon. That was before the fire when her and five of my brothers and sisters got burnt up, and I was sent away, and old Gideon started over; but still it made Laverne my niece. I didn't know. And then when I found out I cried and said, "Please, God," and told her to get off my back. But she just laughed and called me stupid: "You stuu-pid!" Just like that.

Like that party last year at the tournament, I didn't want to go—the team, we had a chance; and me and Dean were forward, guard—he was my man. She called us cowards. Standing on Big Andy's boat in the Prince Rupert harbor, standing at the bow with the cabin lights behind her, yelling "Cowards, Nanoot cowards!" Like on the old war canoes. Until we got afraid someone might hear her, and Dean said, "Come on, Moon, we gotta put Laverne to bed," and started climbing down the ladder from the pier when Big Andy, he was anchored three or four boats out, came reelin' out the cabin door and pulled her in. I didn't want to go, neither did Dean; and when we saw who all was there, we wished we hadn't. Pretty near the whole team, with Coach Andy making toasts against the eighteen rival teams and glancing pretty frequent at his watch (he'd set a curfew), while Crow and Freddy Matson and Berriman and Slim—they'd each one brought a boatload from the village—sat slapping thighs and dipping from a plastic diaper hamper, "Molly's bucket." I started to back out, but Dean was in already and Laverne, perched on Big Andy's knee and singing Crow's song, saw me: "It's Moon!" she cried, "ol' yellow moon. Come on, Moon, do your trick!" And she and Crow started singing while Big Andy, tapping his tin cup with Berriman's, proposed a toast

"To the damndest forward, the most forward . . . Shut up! Crow, Goddamnit! . . . the best damned . . ."

> *"Ooh, Lay me on my mother's steps*
> *Ethel, Ethel,*
> *An' I'll find my way home!"*

Crow harmonized with Laverne from the *Song of Solomon*, 8:2 (it was a wall plaque in his house). ". . . guard too! No offense to you, Charlie," Andy apologized to Hart, "you're damned good too!" and peered forlornly in his cup as Berriman yelled "Set ups!" and roared laughing. Well, it wasn't long after that the lights went out (Coach Andy had them wired to go at midnight), and most of the younger boys left. I wasn't drunk yet, not by a long shot, but when Vina, old Dan's wife, and Mona Matson and Berriman's wife Myrna came over from his boat (they'd been using the bunks till midnight when the basketball boys had to bed down), and young Venita and Annette slipped in without Big Andy noticing, I knew the time had come to go to bed an' if I didn't, I knew tomorrow there'd be hell to pay. I wouldn't've said anything except for Dean, I couldn't see him, so over the racket I said "Le's go, Dean," and started feelin' my way back out around the table . . . "*ooOhh*," Crow, pie-eyed now, was singing, groaning rather, "*LaAay me on my Mootherz steps, aEthul, aEthul . . .*" when Laverne, she must have slipped off Andy's lap 'cause she was sitting on the table when my hand groped for the door, flung her arm around me and hissed, "Coward! Do your trick!" and hiked her skirt so high I was afraid not to—why, she never even gave me time to lose my teeth! "Now I'm sunk," I thought, and heard Mona Matson's giggle, and Berriman get up and start to bellow like a moose; and just about the time I started hunting mushrooms and Laverne, who knew me pretty well by then, reached down and slipped my teeth out, just about that time Dean rocked the boat. The engine roared and the boat rocked, both bow and stern lines broke, and we lurched out of our moorings drunkenly (luckily we were the outside boat), because it turned out Dean'd been in the wheelhouse flashing the spotlight and had spotlighted Danny swimming in the bay.

"PAN!" he shouted through the speaker from the wheelhouse, then: "Man overboard! I think it's Danny!" And in the turmoil after—Berriman stomping, bellowing, his foot caught in the hamper; Big Andy skunk-drunk taking the helm over; and Freddy Matson peeing in the skiff till Dean and me took over and dropped skiff and picked up Danny—in all the turmoil from the time we lurched out of our moorings to pursue our crazy course out in the bay, a drunken boat if ever there was one, until we dragged young Danny sober as a judge and still protesting, pleading in that quiet and strained whisper, "I'm all right, jus' lemme go, I'll be all right," into the skiff and then onto the boat and watched him stand and shake himself off like a dog and walk away, ready, it looked like, to spit in Vina's or anybody else's eye if they said boo—through all that turmoil till Dean tapped me on the shoulder and I had to go with him to drop the skiff, I picked mushrooms.

But *such* mushrooms . . . more like spring leeks they were, or morels, succulent and tender, only slightly musty . . . mushrooms that had never yet been picked! What happened was the boat lurched and before Dean's voice came over the speaker I fell sprawling at the feet of either Annette or Venita, I'm not sure which; and one of them—I don't know to this day—turned slightly so my cheek which had landed on her knee slid up her thigh and then, just about the time Dean's voice startled us and started people running to their posts and Berriman doing his diaper-hamper dance and Freddy Matson fauceting the skiff, just then a tentative, shy quiver in her thighs and gentle fragrance urged me upwards trembling—I was trembling—'cause it seemed that in that moment earth's whole soul and secret of springtime, if I can say that, was concentrated in that blind, dark hole smelling of ginger. It seemed to me the turmoil all around me and behind me—Berriman's and Crow's and Freddy's and the rest—was nothing but their hunting for mushrooms and, just as when you all go mushroom-picking or clam-digging and everybody flanges out and starts to hunt, soon those who can't find any yell to find the quiet ones 'cause they know the quiet ones are finding some, so all their turbulence was a crying-out to get where I knelt quite by accident . . . quietly devouring mushrooms so young and sweet they tasted just like cockles in a clam-bed.

Then Dean came calling me, urgent, and tapped my shoulder and I had to go with him to drop the skiff. I had to drop what I was doing and get busy. If only, I thought to myself then, and again when I saw Freddy Matson peeing off the stern, and often since, if only every man was free to hunt mushrooms, or whatever he liked best, and didn't have to do this busy-work of living. If I had nothin' else to do but pick mushrooms, I'd be happy. Then when we hauled Danny up and he wanted to go back, I thought, he's hunting starfish. Now they've taken me away from picking mushrooms to keep Danny from picking starfish.

That's life though, and since I seen where hunting gets a guy—once Danny found what he was after, and Dean got the urge—I give it up, 'cause it seems a guy ain't never satisfied. I give it up and started playin' straight, the same time Danny started flukin' and Dean fouled out. I say it started then, when Laverne called us both cowards, and Danny went skin-diving, and Coach Andy (although Dean and me got drunk as skunks) wouldn't kick us off the team. He shouldof booted us—just look what happened!

Danny was team captain, with a drunk forward and guard runnin' crazy down the court—the tournament for Christsake!—we had a chance till then. Come huddle, all he'd say was "Keep it cool, keep it cool, and don't shoot when you're covered. Dribble, fake, but don't shoot—keep it cool." One'a the greatest captains in the world, that Danny was! Last quarter with the score tied and we'd both fouled to the limit, Dean and me; last quarter and the rebounds were all elbows above and knees below—foul every time—and Dean fouled out. We were scramblin' around after a rebound, Dean an' me an' three or four of them French guys, when this Frenchie says, "I'm gonna kill you, Indian." "Too bad," I said, and jerked the ball free, I guess that's just the Indian in me; I didn't growl or anything, just said, "Too bad," and passed the ball to Dean. Well, Dean'd heard him and next rebound he came down hard on Frenchie, elbows in his neck, floored him. That gave them extra shots, and Dean fouled out. So now it's just me, Hazen, rubber-legged and sweatin' like a firehose, steamin' down the court and carryin' the ball tucked under like a football—whistles blowin', flags wavin', people screaming from the stands—I forgot that we were playing basketball! And see five guys in shorts red white and blue ahead of me, and think, "That's funny, shorts!" then, "You got to, Hazen, for the team!" With Danny our team-captain shouting Indian behind, and Frenchie figuring no matter what they do the foul's on me, shouting "Un, du, twa" ahead, an' me crazy-drunk and steamin' downcourt like it was a football field and those three big guys like guards flanking a short, squat mascot, Frenchie . . . me lowerin' my head and driving blind. . . . I didn't know the littlest one was a karate-guy. Flipped me over twice. I got the foul.

Coach Andy came out then, boilin', and started arguing the point with the ref when Dean jumped Frenchie from behind. Before Frenchie could flip him, four more Indians piled on the half a dozen Frenchmen. That started people fighting in the stands. Over the loudspeaker somebody said both teams would be disqualified unless the court was cleared at once, and in five, ten minutes play resumed. The two fouls, the ref declared (Coach Andy standing by; the French coach, it turned out, couldn't speak English), cancelled one another out, so that kept me in the game for overtime.

Danny batted me the toss-up and shouted, "Keep it cool!" an' as soon's I got the ball it happened to me, something happened to me . . . changed, I changed. . . . From that moment on, sure as I'm alive and Dean is dyin' and Danny's dead, as sure as they're both gone an' I'm still here, it's been different.

I got the ball and started workin' it downcourt, keeping cool, but they were all around their basket thick as flies. So I moved back to the ten-second line, dribblin', walkin' backwards, an' I said, "Please God. God." And shot like this. It sunk. We got the basket and though we lost the tournament, afterwards, shaking hands, I didn't want to stop. Shaking hands with Frenchie, sayin', "Good game, good game." An' ever since that day, that game, that shot, it's been different. . . . I can make my best shot and it goes in, and that's God, good feelin'; or I can fluke it in, and maybe it sinks in and maybe not. And though a lot has happened since that game and I've fluked plenty, I never lose my teeth like I used to.

Crow

I coulda left this place, but what the hell. Nora asked me once to pimp for her downtown; clients were limited, she said, in Nanootkish, and if she had a few years left she might as well sell out as give away.

"More than a few years," I said, looking her up and down, and said I'd think it over, but first—if she really wanted me to sell the product, could I sample?

"No," she said, "I only want white customers, downtown."

"Damned right!" I said. "Might as well collect with interest for the land they've stolen from us, and the fishing, and our pride, and we only have our bodies left to do it with, naked at that."

"You think it's just the money, don't you, Crow? Well, it isn't."

"Oh," I said, and wasn't sure just what to say, "I see."

And she said, "No, it's not that either." Then she showed me: "You see this?" she said, and turned so I could see the scar-tissue down one side of her throat. "Now feel," she said, and put my fingers to the other side where I could feel hard little lumps under the skin. "It's TB, Crow, but they didn't get it all. I'm supposed to see the Doctor every six months, but I won't, I haven't and I won't. He'll only send me to the San again, I know. And believe me, Crow," she threw back her head and laughed and I realized what made her so attractive, old as she was: it was that scar just like a beauty- or birth-mark, brown on brown, disappearing down into her blouse. That, and her brand of bittersweetness. "Believe me, clients in the San are worse than here. Old guys coughing, and before they're finished they've spit blood all over you, and slime. No, Crow," and she shook her head and shivered her shoulders, "I'm not going down again unless it's on my own, and you go with me."

"I'll think it over," I said, and I did. I calculated what she'd probably bring in, and what it'd be like, how long she was likely to hold out and how long I could hold off sampling. I thought it over, thought it over hard, and decided that no matter how we played the game, the deck was stacked against us. Sure, we might make a pile of money but we'd lose in the long run. I told her that.

"Crow," she said, "you like dying the slow way, only you're afraid of death. But at least you're not afraid of life— that's why I asked you. Look, I'm offering you a long last laugh at all those downtown guys who think they want to live, but really want to die, and haven't got the guts to pull the trigger. . . ."

". . . or the plug," I said.

". . . they haven't got the guts to admit it."

"So you want me to pull their plugs for them?" I said.

"I don't," she said, "they do. They want it bad, so bad they'll pay high for the privilege of dying. Listen, you just let them look at me, then tell them what I've got; they'll pay double, after they've gone home to think it over."

"Yeh, well, maybe," I said.

"You think it over, Crow, think it over hard."

I had to hand it to Nora, she had a way about her that sort of made a fella *want* to die—not right away though, and I guess that's why I turned her offer down. Like she said, I like dying the slow way, which is another way of saying I like living.

Nora's boy, now, young Danny, and Sady's boy, Dean—their problem was they expected too much from life. Me, I take what's coming, and while I never turn none down, I never lean too far to get none either. A proposition is a proposition and just that, not a proposal, and certain types want one, and some the other. And while every woman (and man too) wants sometime to get raped, some insist on leaving the lights on. Like that nurse Lydia. Any ninny with one eye could see she had hot pants and for no one special either, just for kicks. But she's the kind who has to have the lights on, or maybe in a crowded ward, or on the operating table, I don't know; she has to have that added element of danger and detection—sin too probably. So what does Danny do, and Dean?—propose to her! Then run off and shoot themselves because she twitches and it itches and they can't scratch where they want to, they can't switch off the light and stick it to her.

I told them, "Boys," I said, "a woman's like a cat: she screeches till it's over, then she purrs." And Danny (he was sitting there with Hazen and young Dean), Danny said, "Some women, Crow, are different—you'll admit that?" And I said, "Brindle, tabby, alley, different colors, but all cats; all screech and purr unless you cut their tongues out, then they scratch you." And Danny, "You're an animal, Crow." And I: "Maybe so, but so are women, Danny, so are women; and this little persian pedigree you're hot for, so is she." And he: "Shut your goddam mouth, Crow," jumping up, "you shut. . . ." "Easy, boy, have another drink." "Yeh, keep it cool, sport," Hazen chimed in.

It was then Dean who'd been sitting quiet taking it all in (he was playing his cards close), piped out: "Let's settle this once and for all. If you're so sure of what you say, why don't you prove it, Crow?" And to Danny: "Don't you worry, Danny, I'm with *you*."

"Now wait a minute," I began.

The others stared at Dean, Hazen his mouth gaping, Danny starting to protest.

"What do you think, Hazen?" Dean finessed.

Of course Hazen didn't have any face-cards, just a joker: "Yeh, Ye-ah!" he slavered.

"Now wait a minute," I reneged, because I knew my jack of spades was weak beside Dean's queen, and Danny likely had the king. "What the hell is this?" I said, "I'm not you guys' pimp. If Danny's got the itch, I can't scratch for him." And having tossed my jack, I folded. "Not that I've got any doubts," I added, "I'm just not interested."

That should have finished things. But Danny called: "It looks like Crow's backed down, for all his talk. We'll let you save face, Crow," and played his king, covering both Dean's queen and my jack. But he was so cocksure he bumped the pot.

Dean called. "We'll make it worth your while, Crow. However it turns out."

"Yeh, Crow," Hazen passed.

My turn again. "I'm not too anxious, like I told you" (bluffing now) "but you know me, boys, money talks."

"Yeh," Hazen chimed in, "put chur money where yer mouth is, sport!"

And Danny: "You're bluffing, Crow, but you're covered. Show or shut up."

So I tossed it then, I don't know why, the ace I always carry. Just for the hell of it I called: "Two weeks, two hundred bucks, and no hard feelings. What's your pleasure?"

"An' a booze-flight at the end, if you make out," cried Hazen (he was working then, at Carter's), and slapped a hundred dollars on the table.

Look at it this way: it was a challenge, wasn't it? Something to do. Not that it was worth doing, but what is? It appealed to me, the challenge if not Lydia herself; but she's a woman, isn't she—what more can a man ask? The only thing I sweated was the time, two weeks is short, and a woman has to do it in her mind first—has to lie awake a night or two ahead, dreading the deed, and a night or two after, savoring it. So when I asked her a few days ahead to Milly's birthday party (she and my wife worked together at the hospital), I knew she'd lie awake, I knew she'd come.

"On one condition," she said.

"No, not that," I groaned.

"Why not?" she teased, and her eyes danced.

"Well, from midnight on it's Indian-time," I told her, "so from midnight to sun-up you're on your own, no guarantees. You might even go Indian, who knows?"

"You're on!" she cried. "So long as you teach me to Indian-dance!"

"Well . . . sure," I said, "why not? Only," eyeing her uniform, "not in that outfit."

"Don't worry, Crow, it's a birthday party, isn't it? I'll come dressed."

So she was coming like I knew she would. I knew Milly would have to leave to go on shift, too, around midnight; Danny would most likely dog his sweetheart's tracks, but she might ditch him, or Vinny his step-mother might divert him, or he might pass out—leaving the last dance to Old Crow.

That's how I planned it more or less, but it didn't work exactly out to plan. First, Vinny got too drunk; then Lydia went home when Milly left at midnight, Danny sniffing up the boardwalk behind them; then everybody got too drunk. I'd finally resigned myself to do my little bit by Vinny, though she was too drunk to know or care, when all of a sudden Danny—the kid was unbalanced, I always thought so—comes dashing in the smokehouse like a houseafire, tells me I'm not his father (whoever said I was?) and dashes out again, yelling at Lydia, who wrapped in a foxfur had followed him: "Get out! Get out of here!" With that he dashes off half-cocked in the cold dark.

Vinny's swimming on the smokehouse floor right out of it when in pops Lydia, fire-red hair flying, falling back in the direction Danny ran as if the breeze he stirred were fanning it, still on she comes and sees in the half-light, first Vinny struggling half-dressed to her feet, then me in the half-shadow loitering, and steps in full.

"Well, blow me down," she says, "Old Sharp has laid his thousands, but Old Crow his ten thousands, eh, Old Crow?" And without waiting for reply flings off the foxfur and, ask Vinny, if she had a stitch on, that was all she had, one of those sheer things they wear to bed. She stared into the fire then raised her arms up, started shimmyin' and said, "Teach me to Indian-dance, Crow!"

"What?" I said.

"Indian-dance!" she cried, shimmyin' with her arms, her legs, and I mean every curve beneath that see-through shift. "This is the night!"

"It sure is," I agreed, and held my arms out, dangling my elbows like broken wings—she dangled hers; I bent my knees and shwooshed my hips and started shuffling the "Old Man of the Woods"; she bent her knees and shwooshed and shuffled too. Across the fire we shuffled, glowering. I went into the Eagle step, she kept the broken-wing: around the fire, pursuing, circling, retreating; Vina swimming upward to her feet, gaping.

"Well, I'll be damned," she gasped. "Well, I'll be damned!" then grabbed two billets of driftwood to beat dance-time: *Bump*-bump bump-bum, *Bump*-bump bump-bum. . . . "*Aleeya gwaacom aihyah, aleeya ay gwaacom,*" *Bump*-bump bump-bum, "*Aleeya ay gwaacom aihyah kwacom aihyah kwacom. . . .*" Vina closed her eyes and put her whole soul in it, swaying as she beat and sang; it was one of her own people's songs I'd never heard before. I didn't understand a word. "*Kwacom ayhlajah toulisah quatno. . . .*" Bump-bump, *Bump*-bump. . . . The tempo quickened.

"What's it saying?"—Lydia, breathing short and flagging somewhat, swaying just in front of me.

"It says, *Lay your heart down to the ground.*" I put my hand to my ear, as if listening, "*Throw your feathers off, and Father-fish will come to you.* Like this," I showed her, kneeling down on knees and elbows, but keeping my hips swaying. "And keep your eyes closed," I commanded.

She knelt down, swaying still those lovely white hips bare except for the chemise, and while Vinny kept the rhythm up, and while I prayed the Salmon-god (whose song it may have been, who knows?) that it would prove a long-drawn-out song as befits so big a fish, I scampered round the fire on hands and knees till beneath the hanging racks of sockeye—boneless, finless, slit from the tail up but not beheaded, eyeless though—I positioned myself eye to keyhole with that beautifully upended, slightly moist and distended white rear-end, swaying all the while and slowly, ever so slowly, I touched its mouth and knew from the wet kiss it gave, the god was ready.

"Father-Salmon, Father-Salmon," I started whisper-chanting, and from its mouth nearer the dust, its other mouth which had been moaning to rhythm while this one swayed, the whisper-chant was taken up: "Father-Salmon, Father-Salmon, come, O come to me; O come to me, O Father-Salmon come." And Father-Salmon, just as though he'd heard the prayer, slipped from the rack above and slid inside, nosing his red fish-flesh little by little just as he prows his way up spawning streams. From ocean to ocean he slid, fire to fire and earth to earth, and as he slid the swaying stopped, but not the song, not the driftwood rhythm; as he slid the invocation stopped, but not the god. He kept on sliding, probing, burying himself until the cave cried, the amazed grave opened, and the conscious other-end cried, "Christ! What are you using?" and reared bolt upright, then quickly knelt again as if in pain. "What in God's name. . .?" a weak and baffled whimper. "Stop it, stop. . . ." trailing into muffled sobbings in the dust.

I drew him out, the Ancient and Most Deep, and tossed him on the fire, a sacrifice; while gingerly, most gingerly this most-favored-among-women drew herself together and, past Vinny who was nodding at her drums, limped out into the cold dark foxfur night.

You think I should feel bad? I don't. I'll tell you why.

> *Ten little Indians standing in a line;*
> *One came home and then there were nine.*

We started singing that in the late forties, after the last war when the Indians were lost—this time we were lost, no doubt about it; the colored peoples of the world had encircled the whites who had encircled us, but the whites had broken through again, and we were lost. Sitting in the bar at Ocean Falls beneath the goat-head, the goat-head Jesse Blackstock shot which had turned brown with nicotine, sitting singing celebrating— not the winning of the war, but the new Indian Act which allowed us to buy liquor—four little Indians singing. While miners and loggers and fishermen, ex-soldiers or sailors, sang "Ninety-nine bottles of beer on the wall," and worked their way down or passed out, we sang "Ten little Indians standing in a line; One came home and then there were nine." We sang and we couldn't stop singing: because the one who came home came home in a box, and he was Hap Blackwood, our buddy. . . .

We, the Wilderness

> *Nine little Indians swinging on a gate;*
> *One fell off and then there were eight.*

Lots of us had fallen off, but when Kaleb cried, "Badeagle, it's Badeagle, by God!" we sang "Nine little Indians" till we were dry. Hell, all of us were falling off the wagon all the time, but when Bird fell off that last time in Vancouver he fell flat; the bus driver didn't even bother to slow down, the gutter was so filled with trash, he just slid in and over—bump, bump—on. Unfortunately, Bird didn't die . . . not right away. . . .

> *Eight little Indians went to Heaven;*
> *One said he'd stay and then there were seven.*

"That sure sounds like the tale of the eight little kids who got lost, an' it winter, an' they jumped in a fire and got found, but the one who jumped first got burnt up. I've heard my ol' man tell that tale," Big Andy said. "I heard it too," said Glennie, "only the one that jumped first was the dog." Kaleb laughed. "Don't that remind you of Theron?" he said. "Now there was a crazy Indian. . . ."

Theron Jameson was one of seven or eight boys the Mormons took away to school. When they sent them back, Theron talked a lot about lost tribes, and how a prophet wasn't without honor except in his own home-town. He was right, because pretty soon Samson Starr caught him with Baby, though Theron had his own wife by that time. Theron said Brigham somebody in the Bible had had twenty-seven wives, and that was what had kept him young. Samson said he could quote scripture too, and grabbed a bear-skull the dogs had drug up from the beach and clobbered Theron. Baby jumped in then and kicked Samson in the groin, then she and Theron ran off to Utah. They sent Samson a postcard with a church picture on the front, and on the back it said: "He that is wounded in the stones, or hath his

privy member cut off, shall not enter into the congregation of
the righteous. (Deut. 23:1). Love, Baby." That shook Samson up
some, and he cried a lot; Sharon Jameson cried a lot too, then
they cried together. They weren't going to get married legally
till they found out a ship's captain could do it.

"So where does that put Heaven?"—Glennie. "Salt Lake
City, eh, Kaleb?" "Depends on where you been," he said, staring
in his glass, "and how badly you been burnt."

> *Seven little Indians playing funny tricks;*
> *One took a ride and then there were six.*

"I guess that's when Darryl and Brodie and them went horsing
around Blind Man's Bluff," Big Andy said. "Just what did happen?" I asked, "was it the oarlocks?" "Nah, it was just the current," Kaleb said. "You know yourself how they've logged off
all the trees along the bank? Well, those boys probably remembered berrypickin' there as kids and boating with their families,
before the pulp mill came in." "Yeah!" said Glennie, "thimble-
berries, blueberries, and blackberries by the ton there—my
Granny used to take me as a kid!" "Well, now there's no small
brush to break the current," Kaleb said. "No berries either,"
Glennie added glumly; and Big Andy whose son Darryl was
said, "Christ! Can't you guys sing?"

> *Six little Indians learning how to dive;*
> *One swam away and then there were five.*

My turn this time, though each of us had someone. My own
son, Hartley, by my first wife; though Glennie'd lost a brother,
and Kaleb a best friend, and Andy his son Darryl—all by
drowning. So many! Some lost so completely that not even their
bodies were recovered. In front of nearly every house one grave-
marker read "lost at sea, his body was not found," and those
that did wash up were better lost.

We, the Wilderness

Five little Indians peeping through a door;
One ran behind and then there were four.

That door, said Glennie who'd lost his first wife in childbirth, his mother to TB, and a son with a ruptured appendix, that door he said was to the operating room: whoever went behind never returned.

Four little Indians climbed up in a tree;
One slid down and then there were three.

This actually happened, only there were two of them, not four. Magnus Blackwater's son, Simon, after a full night spent up a tree away from wolves, slid down at daybreak and got eaten with young Roddie Gladstone looking on. But Andy said, "Hell, you guys wanta know why we adopted? It's cause I landed on a branch when I was ten. Right there!" he said, and didn't seem too pleased when we all laughed.

Three little Indians out in a canoe;
One hopped out and then there were two.

There was a curious silence when we sang that the first time sitting in the bar in Ocean Falls, our table littered with spent soldiers and dead butts, the air heavy with our breathing and remembering . . . a curiously sober silence. Kaleb checked his watch and stretched. "I guess it's getting on near closing time," he said, and scratched. "Yeah, I guess so," Glennie or Andy agreed. But they all three sat there till I nodded toward the goathead browned over the years with nicotine, the goathead bagged and mounted and presented as a token of the Indians' good-will and tribute to the pulp-mill by the last of the old blood-chiefs and the first of the deserters, Jesse Blackstock, son of Stone Blackstock, grandson of Chief Black Stone—*The* Chief.

Nobody made a move to pay or go, so I said, "What the hell, you guys, we all know who that is." "Yeah, I guess so," they said, "I guess we do." "We've got this far, might's well finish it," I said, emptying the remains of the last bottle in our glasses. "Yeah, might's well," Kaleb said, "go on to two." That took me by surprise. "What's the matter with you guys?" I said. "Are you afraid to name a traitor because he betrayed something you believe in, or because he got away scot-free and you wish you could?" Kaleb glared. "Got away, hell!" he shot back. "What? To be Cabbage-King and Chief-Looney at the nuthouse? Why, the guy deserves our pity if he weren't such a disgrace, chief or no chief." He tossed his whiskey off and wiped his mouth. "So it's that he betrayed something you believe in," I prodded, and as soon as I'd said it, and remembered that Chief Jesse was Kaleb's father-in-law, I wished I hadn't.

But I had. Glennie and Andy were watching Kaleb like you'd watch a bear, respectful of his strength, uncertain which way he might head next. Glennie I noticed had slid down a little in his chair; Andy swallowed, ve-ry cautiously. "It's not what I believe in," Kaleb very quietly replied. "It's what I am. Not what I chose to be either. I never had a choice, and neither did you, Crow, neither did you, Andy, or you, Glennie. We're what we are, maybe not what we were meant to be, but what we are; Jesse Blackstock isn't even that. He's not an Indian, he's not a white man either; he not even a half-breed—he's nothing. For what it's worth, I pity him; but here's what I think of him—" He spit. While Glennie regarded through lidded eyes and cigarette smoke, slumped in a sort of trance, the brown saliva slide down the brown bottle side and slowly come to rest on the scarred table, Kaleb energetically shoved back his chair and went to the men's room. The spittle settled. "I wonder why he did it?" Glennie asked, without removing either eyes or cigarette. "Who knows?" Andy answered, "some guys get funny notions about the outside. I guess Chief Jesse . . ." "No, I mean

Kaleb," Glennie said, "that's not like him. I wonder if it's anything to do with his being married to Sady?" "Go on to two," I said, "before he gets back."

> *Two little Indians playing in the sun;*
> *One fell asleep and then there was one.*

"That sure sounds like First-man and First-woman," Andy said, "I've heard my old man tell that story." "Yeah," said Glennie, "Menigula and Peacemaker, the first pair." "Which one of 'em was it fell asleep?" Kaleb asked as he sat down. "Peacemaker, man! Sure, after ol' Menigula had made a bark canoe, and towed a killer-whale in by a kelp-line, and struck fire from a fire-stick, and built a longhouse, and give 'er all the comforts of the coast, Peacemaker just lay down and fell asleep on him one day." "But not till after she had filled the longhouse with lots of kids," I added Laughing. "And drawn the war-canoes from other tribes—she was that pretty," Andy said. Kaleb nodded seriously. "Umph," he said.

> *One little Indian playing all alone;*
> *He went in and then there were none.*

"Well, here's to us," I said, and we clinked glasses. "And to our kids," said Kaleb, "may they never know what it feels like to be 'last man.' " And we clinked glasses once again, and drained the dregs. And now he's here still, and I'm here still, and our kids have gone before us: he's losing Dean, and he lost Brucie before that, and Louisa his daughter living downtown with some white guy, lost her too. While Sady, his peacemaker (if you could call her that), lay down and fell asleep on him ten years ago. . . . And me? Well I lost two kids, little ones, while drunk: fell on top of them and smothered them. That was after my first wife, no peacemaker either, left me and tried to take them with her and we quarreled—lost her too. And another one by drowning—accident—and who knows what will come of my kids by my second wife . . . who knows?

Kaleb's at least smart, he stayed single after Sady. I might as well have because, children or no children, married or not, sometimes I feel like that "One little Indian, playing all alone," playing with myself and the game really doesn't matter, it really doesn't matter who walks in or who walks out since nothing is gained anyway, and nothing lost. . . .

Kaleb

They all come back, keep coming, to torment a man; the farther on you go it seems the further back you get, and nothing should surprise anyone—I tell myself that—nothing should catch anyone off-guard. Because, like Nature, humankind repeats itself, and like God Himself must, man gets tired of comings and goings. Why, even the sea gets tired reclaiming land, and the land gets even tireder, wears away.

I am mumbling to myself now, having just come home from Dean's room, watching him struggle with the sea. He is losing, little by little he is giving way; soon the sheet will cover his face also, he will sink. But his body will float back and his face will be uncovered, the face of a little boy, trusting, bright, to ask me questions neither I nor anybody else could ever answer except, maybe, in the moment of dying. Maybe I'll say, when he asks "Where's my Mommy gone to?" I'll say, "Son, you tell me, you should know." Or if he asks, "Why are you still here, and she's gone off?" I'll say, "I wish I weren't here, son, and I wish she were." No, no new answers from the land of the living, and no new secrets from the country under waves; just the same old traffic to and fro, the same old questions without answers.

"They're coming. We passed them on the way up." Janet, she is out of breath from walking; Polly, her daughter from downtown, comes in behind her, lays her hand on my hand, I nod back. "Everything ready?" Janet looks around. Polly takes her coat off while her mother fiddles with the stove, checks the coffee Laverne perked, and lifts the napkin off the plate of sandwiches, sniffs them, asks, "This enough?", then tucks the napkin back and takes her coat off; they sit down. Josh passes from the store-front to the little room just off the kitchen, seats himself at the old roll-top where he does accounts; he shuffles accounts lists and commences work. His back is to us in the open door. Old Gideon, lying out of sight in the iron poster, snuffles a little and starts coughing; Josh passes him the spittoon and he hacks, spits, sighs. Through the open door we can hear his every movement but he can't hear anything, yet he's the one the Pentecostals asked if they could come.

We sit. Polly leans to me and whispers, "How was he tonight?"

"Same," I answer, "Sharp says not to get our hopes up."

"Oh," she says, and we sit quietly, hearing the labored sound of the old man's breathing, Josh rustling his papers, and through the blanket draped between where we sit and the back-room, Baby Michael's whining before dropping off. Then Hazen and Laverne come in and sit down.

We're all here now, gathered here in memory of Dean before he's gone. Because he's going, and they're coming, and we're here. That's why we're gathered. Before the sightless face is covered and the covered body carried out of the hospital into the church. From the church to the boat, from the boat to Grave Island, from Grave Island to the country underwaves. And all around, above too, it will be raining then as always. Now we're waiting, gathered here in memory of someone not yet passed, but passing as we all are on a way familiar to us all, as familiar as though we'd all passed on ourselves: waiting, watching, dying all of us though none of us has actually died but only rehearsed dying—from the village to Grave Island, from Grave Island to the village; from hospital to church, and church to hospital, back again—coming, going on the surface but afraid to step out of the boat or off the boardwalk, rehearsing it so often it haunts us, they haunt us who have passed on and come back, keep coming back in dreams and memories to haunt and call us cowards: "*Coward! let me go,*" she wails, "*you're married to a corpse! You who'd spew your guts to any slut while I was living. Unbind me, let me go back to the sea . . . !*"

". . . Kaleb, Kaleb. They're coming, Kale."

"No! . . . What? Oh, thanks, Hazen. There's more chairs in the store-room, could you . . .? Hullo, Moses. Hazen's getting some more chairs. Huh? Oh, 'bout the same. Sharp says not to get our hopes up."

"The ways of the Lord are not our ways, Kaleb, remember that. Our ways are not His way. But we'll praise the Lord as long as we have breath, and He will change our ways and mend our broken bones and put a new song in our hearts, even 'Praise His Name Forever!' "

"—Amen!" Stanley on the steel-guitar dutifully seconds Moses and the bull. They're here, all right; Letty and the Ravens too, already settling down around the corpse to croak amens: "Praise His wonderful name!" "Juh-*Eeze*-us, Juh-*Eeze*-us!" "Prechus Jesus!"

Pastor Moses takes his seat beside the door, grave and prayerful, wetting with the pink tip of his tongue those bloodless lips whenever anybody enters. Thin, grim, pale, Bible and chorus-book in hand, and wearing the same stiff double-breasted suit he always wears—where from but the Southern States? Where else but to the Indians? A few stragglers arrive talking and laughing and shaking out umbrellas on the porch. They open the door on Pastor Moses' blanched foreboding face; all talking ceases as they tip-toe past.

Huu-aAaang!—the warning chord from Stanley's steel-guitar. Moses' tongue flicks twice in rapid-fire. "Aa-*Men!*" cries Letty.

"I think we're all here, praise the Lord!" Moses leaps up to his feet. "Brother Stanley, if'n that praise-GEEtar of your'n is plugged in, start us off with washed-in-th'-blood, O I'm washed-in-th'-prechus-blood o' JEEsus; Number seventy-four, folks, an' does everybody have a hymnbook? Here's some more to pass around, Sister Leticia."

Letty hands out hymnbooks while Pastor Moses look on, wets his lips, and leans to confer briefly with Deacon Harper, first lieutenant, second in command. Harp's wearing the orange sweatshirt he's been wearing since his trip downtown, inscribed with bold black letters: REPENT and underneath the curling black lines dangling from each letter (which coil together at the bottom in a kind of snake's head), in tiny, tiny type: "made in Calif., U.S.A." Harp hunches forward on his chair, all three hundred weight, returning Moses' hissed commands with unctuous grunts and whispers. Occasionally they glance at me; I nod. Now Moses straightens up. While Harp sinks back and begins thumbing through his hymnbook, Moses trains on me two glittering eyes and flicks his tongue. I turn like Harp to *Choruses of Hope and Consolation.*

"Hold it! Brother Stan, there must be thirty of us here now, but there's some more folks passing. Call them in, Brother Simon, call them in to the healing of the Centurion's son! He had great faith, Kaleb, great faith, and if you have faith to match his faith, faith the size of a grain of mustard-seed, a tiny little mustard-seed—" Moses holds up thumb and forefinger and just about the time several voices "amen," Josh shuts the side-room door and Baby Michael, awakened by the steel guitar, begins screaming from the backroom while Moses starts, and everybody with him, singing

We, the Wilderness

> *Washed in the blu-ud,*
> *Washed in the blu-ud,*
> *I'm washed in the pre-chus blud of*
> *Juh-ee-eez-zus!*

Laverne got up and left to quiet Michael, Hazen with her, while Janet jumped to fiddle with the stove and check the coffee, then left by the side entrance carrying a pail. That left Polly and me and the Pentecostals. They swung right on without pause into

> *Who is on the Lord's side*
> *Who will fight the foe?*

Polly stole a glance to tell me she was on my side, then raised her hymnbook to eye level while I sat there. It looked like a long evening ahead.

After a few opening choruses and multiple amens, Pastor Moses turned the program over to Deacon Harper. Harp was to field hymn requests, interspersing words of comfort, prayer, and dedication, then turn the program back to Pastor Moses for the sermon. This was the pattern. But tonight, you could tell, they had something else in mind, you could tell Harp was working up to something when he kept talking between hymns about ". . . a balsam of comfort, a healing balsam which we see arightly rightaway the scales fall from our eyes, we know we haven't got, but who has? Who has? That is a question in your hearts, in his heart too, strong-hearted in his reaching out, he's reaching out, but where? That is a question in our hearts tonight as we sing 'Will your anchor hold?' And let us think about the family, Kaleb, Hazen and Laverne, the family and the great centurion, let us think about them while we sing this strong heart hymn. Stanley—"

Will your anchor hold in the storms of life?
When the clouds unfold they-er wings of strife;
When the strong tides life and the cables strain,
Will your anchor dri-ift or-er firm remain?

We have an anchor that keeps the soul . . . !

So they all sang and thought about us, and we thought about them thinking about us and didn't sing, and everybody wondered where the great centurion fit in. Then it was Pastor Moses' turn to talk again.

"Folks, we been thinking tonight about that great centurion, about how his young lad was healed by such great faith Jesus said he hadn't seen such great faith in all of Jewry. (*Amen.*) An' while we been sitting here thinking, singing and thinking, another young lad's lying dying in hospital, no more'n a stone's throw away! Now, I ask you, is that right? (*Right! Brother.*) No, it's wrong! Because it shows what little faith we have, you have, I have. It shows what little faith we have in Jesus. Now," (holding up his hand), "if that centurion was here he'd come to Jesus (*Come to Jesus!*), he wouldn't go to medical science—medical science can't help him. He wouldn't go to the Anglicans either! (*Amen.*) 'Cause they don't care, they don't care about the Indians. Now" (holding up his hand) "Jesus didn't care for the Romans, that's what they say; he said 'Render unto Caesar,' and they twist that—NO! the truth is Jesus didn't care if that centurion was Roman, no more'n he cares that this young lad's Indian—it doesn't matter to him, JESUS (*Amen*), not at all. No," (holding up his hand) "if Brother Kaleb here had faith, great faith in Christ like that centurion, it wouldn't matter. . . ."

I guess Josh had in mind to rescue me, and had been listening the whole time behind the door; anyway, when it sounded like any minute my faith might be put to the test, Josh opened the sidedoor and motioned for me. This disrupted things and distracted Pastor Moses so that by the time I was safely into the next room he'd called another hymn and they were singing. "Brother Josh—" I said fondly as he sat down at the roll-top. "Brother, Hell!" he whispered, "I was scared you might actually *do* it—fall down on your knees and *confess* or somethin'!" I clapped him on the shoulder and eased down on the iron-poster (Old Gideon was wheezing regularly, asleep). "I *was*," he protested, "you're under strain; 'sides, confessin' at your age might prove disastrous—to *me!*" He resumed checking debits against credits while I looked on idly over his shoulder. At the bottom and in pencil he jotted under credits, "Kept Brother from Brethren," and under debits, "Kept Brother from Sistern"; between the two he wrote "Paid in Full" and cancelled out both entries.

"For keeping me from marriage all these years," he whispered grinning. "Me?" I said. "Why, Sady tried to line you up, and haven't I always said . . .?" "Screw your preachments, brother; and for that matter," he added wistfully, "Sady's matches. Yes, ah yes. No, it's your negative example that's seen me through the years and weirs of women's wiles, your example's kept me from the hole, ah, cistern, at least from gettin' stuck there—that's true religion. Example—and tonight's a small back-payment, not a loan. After all," he grinned, "I'm more good Steward than Samaritan." "And more good Jew than Indian," I added as with black and red-lead pencils Josh tallied and transcribed some figures onto a clean sheet, shoved up from the roll-top, and taking a deep breath cracked the door. Steel-guitar and singing flooded in:

Oo, how precious the thought that we all may recline,
Like John the belov-ed and blest,

On Jesus' strongarm, where no tempest can harm,
    Secure in the Ha-ven of Rest!
O-oo—

And Josh, debts and credits in hand, catty-cornered tiptoe through the kitchen to the store-front. He nodded briefly in passing Pastor Moses, Deacon Harper, and Sister Leticia whose chairtop, tilted back against the front door, had got wedged in under the doorknob. Josh panicked briefly, wrestling it loose, finally got the door open and turning, made a stage-bow to them all, then disappeared to his sanctum. The praise-guitar and chorus swelled across his wake and poured in through the door he'd left ajar where Gideon wheezing slept and I sat drowning.

O I've anchored my soul in the Haven of Rest,
    I'll sail the wide seas no more;
Tho' the tempest may sweep o'er the wild, stormy deep,
    In Je-sus, I'm safe, ever-mo-er.

I couldn't help thinking about Sady. All my life I've been a sentimental sort, and certain songs and taverns and especially old photos bring it on. I grow morose and sad thinking about the Indian people and their past, or worse, thinking about Sady. There's such unlimited scope for nostalgia for an Indian, and so little ground for hope, no wonder Indians like sitting around drinking because it loosens tongues and joggles memories and starts them pow-wowing about the Great Days Gone. (You'll never hear an Indian talk much about the future, no further than this coming summer's fishing; if you do, buy him a beer or two and he'll come 'round.) Anyway, old photos start me reminiscing, such as this picture I saw once of two Indians, South American, buck naked though there was deep snow all around; the caption read, "Last of a Noble Race." That was at Dr. Sharp's place. There's one they have in a Prince Rupert pub run by a German, showing four or five Europeans with rifles and a burnt-out hut in front. The caption I wrote down and got a German nurse to translate: *"Julio Popper mit seiner Truppe auf ein Indianerjag, 1885."* That moved me too.

And certain songs (especially hymns) always get to me, and, bad music though it was, it was that same hymn *Haven of Rest* that they were singing long ago at another wake just like now, while I sat in this room with the door ajar, like now sitting, watching—not the photo of Sady on the wall that I see now above the artificial flowers, but the woman in black framed by the roses of her dead first husband's coffin . . . sitting, sweating, hearing the same hymn and watching the same woman, more beautiful in black than in her wedding-gown, more womanly as widow than as wife . . . sweating, dreading to tell her how it came to pass that I was here with her and Lloyd was dead.

Because she had gotten up in the middle of that service, in the middle of that hymn *Haven of Rest* and caught and held my eye and came to me in this little room and closed the door (only it stayed jarred a little, just like now), and said, "Now, Kaleb, tell me now." Because I had said, "Sady, he died in my arms, Sady. The last thing I said to him was I'd look after you, and then he died."

"You're positive he's dead?"

She must have read it in my eyes as I started to answer about the storm, the sea, the seine-boat keeled completely over with four crewmen clinging to its ribs, her husband off the bow dog-paddling. . . .

"He couldn't swim," she said, waiting my reply, "he never learned."

It must have mirrored in my eyes the way she watched me, fascinated like a little girl might watch a film and wet her pants she feels so scared, but secure too knowing it's not real or, if it's happened, it's not happening to *her;* seeing in my eyes and hearing in my silence the whole scene and story in a moment, in a snap:

"You're the only one can swim, Kale," Happy talking, and me stripping my big woolen pants and shirt. Jumped or dived, I can't remember, then wrestling that three-inch anchor line around us. Twice he floundered, twice I gave him up, finally towed him in tandem to the skiff. Eben Sandy swam right past us to the pile of floating cork-line. That was the last time anyone saw *him!* Me meanwhile struggling with Lloyd on the skiff, him coughing, gagging, me trying to pump him but he wouldn't throw up properly and the waves were breaking on us and I told him when I saw fear in his eyes I'd look after Sady for him, then I lost him. Lost him once, first time, a big breaker washed him over and I dove down after him and brought him back. Lost him again, quite a-ways down when I saw him sink the second time, dove down and came up with him and the skiff bouncing around . . . skiff banged me on the neck, nearly lost him. Swallowed quite a bit of water but I managed to grab hold and come up underneath the skiff for air. I still had my arm around him—breaker coming, so I shoved him to one side and I'm clawing the skiff-keel as far as I could reach, breaker hit and flipped the skiff rightside, washed us both. I had to swim back, dive down, locate him again and bring him back. Got him on the skiff and saw this little rope, cork line, grabbed it and tied it on his wrist, then let him go. He never sank again, he never sank once I secured him. I knew he was dead then, had been all the while: I had been rescuing a corpse while three men drowned.

"I'm positive," I said to her, "he's dead, and so are Ralph, and Happy, and the Skipper. Ralph rode the net, and Happy and the Skipper rode the ship down. Lloyd was with me in the skiff."

"He's dead," she said again, this time not so much for the

fact as for the sound and feel of it: "He's dead," looking away from me towards the door where *Haven of Rest* was being sung.

"I told him I'd look after you," I hesitated, "and I will, Sady, I will."

She looked at me and spoke, I still remember, softly, for the door was still ajar, but flat, without a trace of emotion, as though these were the facts, take them or leave them, he was dead. "I'm no good, Kaleb. If you want me you can have me, I'm yours from the moment he died. No need for marriage, unless you want that too, I consider myself married—to you now. And I'll be faithful, as faithful as you are. But I'm no good, Kaleb, I tell you now."

I took her in my arms (hers hung loosely at her sides) and kissed her lips—no urgency, no passion, no quick-fear. "I told him I'd take care of you, and I will, Sady," I said, "I swear I will!"

"Marry me, and you're married to a corpse," she said. And such was our marriage ceremony, with the blackbird of the storm for priest, and the wake from a sinking boat in the next room which was to be her kitchen and our bedroom till she died.

An angel in the kitchen and a devil in bed . . .? Well, she was neither either place. By day she stood up to the stove while Josh and I and Father, and later on the children, sat around the table breakfasting, or lunching, or dining, hours on end. When we would sit around after meals and play crib, Josh and I, or when Old Gideon stayed to read his Bible, Sady it seemed was always standing at the stove—poking at the fire, or heating water, doing dishes, getting food for the next meal (after the babies came she never sat)—as though she and the old castiron were of one unflinching metal: when the stove was off she lay down straight, when the stove was on she stood. At night she slept; and Josh, lying in the bed which was later to be Dean's, lying awake listening late into the night, listening in a sweat of fear and resentment as though he were the one being deprived, listened in vain for sounds of what he called "creating" (he also called it that when the children woke up screaming), however long or hard he listened or lay there. Except for a brief spell every Spring — it always happened—as soon as we went out for herring-spawn and seaweed, Sady flushed to life and filled the boat, the shore, the ocean—her kitchen could no longer contain her. As though the ocean was her garden and lay fallow all winter and the house her pantry or root-cellar. But come Spring—sap and sunlight, wilderness and warm sea—out she rushed, hungry, to pick seaweed and gather spawn and pluck up abalone at low tide. Nothing could confine her, gale warning or ground swell, and no one. Her hunger owed its life not to the sun (she was even more avid hunting abalone in a storm, surf pounding as she sliced them off the rocks). And as her hungering was for no less than all of Nature—any plant or animal, medicinal or edible, might in a trice become her prey—so her hankering in those moments when, flushed from the hunt and bearing a full sack she reboarded from her skiff, was for whomever happened to be there to help her up, hold fast her sack, and watch her pour her seahaul on the deck and then, exhausted, lie down on a cushion of wet seaweed, arms spread-eagled, her sole garment a cloth shift long since drenched and dropped about the hips as too confining, eyes shut against the sun and sliding bare brown legs over the oozy mass for the tingly sensation it afforded.

Many's the time I've seen her reach a climax just like that, without any help from me or anything except the sun, seawater, and salt air, and the barnacled seaweed she lay on, bedded in; and many more's the time I've covered her while she, without ever opening her eyes, made me feel the pure sensation of sun on my back and slime and seaweed round my legs and trembling flesh. Then the term "creating" seemed to fit. If later I'd ask how it felt all by herself, and if it was as good alone, she'd smile—just like she did when Dean was born—"Some Indian!" she'd tease, and lean to kiss me.

Those were our best times together, every spring when she'd "go Indian" and let Nature be her lover and I'd slip in at the last minute and feel some of the vibrations between her and the sun and the sea and the fresh dulce. . . . Hot breath, flat belly, taut brown breasts and thighs that softened, opened, and enclosed as, scratching me like seaweed and clinging like abalone, Sady caught and cherished sun and sperm at herring-spawn-time. Oh, I made sure I was ready and the boat and all ship-shape. The day gulls started screeching and we saw quick-silver stipples, I'd already hiked up in the woods and cut a cedar-tree for spawn while Josh had hung his sign 'spawn' on the store-front and taken to his bed days and lying awake nights. She was that sudden, seasonal (all our kids have birth-days in December!)—so that between Sady and me and the herringspawn Josh heard enough "creating" every spring to last all winter.

Spring was Sady's season, autumn's mine. When salmon season's over and you get up venison, maybe a goat from Rivers Inlet where there's snow on the high-ground; the rains return and more and more you sit around indoors and gain your weight back and, except for the odd day jigging cod and halibut, you put your boat up. There's money too, from fishing, so you drink while she jars salmon and salts venison and puts away the roe and silt for stink-eggs and trout-bait. That's how I sentimentalize the years that passed, the springs and falls that disappeared like herring down a loon's throat, like stink-eggs turning on the shelf. . . . Because autumn turns to winter, spring to summer, and you turn too, and she turns, till the freshness that was spring and the ease of autumn you remember become gorged and glutted in the sixteen-hour-a-day seven-day-a-week salmon cannery assembly line and the mindless, aimless week-long drunks of endless winter, summer. . . .

. . . till you're slavering and singing and before you know it, at a party you've been at four, five, six, seven days (hell, Crow had a booze-flight, didn't he?) you find you're up in someone (who? now, was it Milly, or Vina, or . . . it doesn't matter). It doesn't matter that you can't do anything, that like a weak earthworm you're slavering instead, you're in her, that's the point, and you turn round and the song which wasn't much of a song anyway dries on your lips and chin, because *she's* there and she's been there watching, waiting for you to turn, watching you turn autumn into winter, endless winter. . . .

. . . till she's stained and spattered with the blood and gore of fish she's picked up off the chain and torn the guts out of all day, standing beside sixty other fishstained women, tired as they, too tired to go to sleep, and when you wake up the next morning she's still sitting and you notice the vanilla extract bottles but not, at first, the other because she's blood-stained from the fish, only it's not dry, but fresh, and it's not fishblood but her own; you notice then she's bleeding from the wrists and that's the first time, the first summer you recall that wasn't followed by and didn't follow spring. . . .

We were living in the summer-quarters, long lines of army barracks the cannery had taken over at Blind Channel, without toilets, one cot to a compartment, no running water. It was crowded, even though Laverne and Dean were both downtown at residential school (she was in grade four, he in grade three), and baby Louisa stayed at Sady's mother's, Nora's place. I was fishing, though the fishing weeks were only two days long, the "weekends" five, so I was in more than I was out, with nothing to do but mend net and get drunk while

We, the Wilderness

Sady worked. Worked sixteen hours daily, everyday. It wasn't the first summer we'd done it, and we weren't the only family doing it—pretty nearly all the families in Nanootkish, every year. . . . But this was the first summer without a beginning or an end, without a spring of getting ready and a fall of easing off; and I felt it every time I walked the longporch home, passing crowded compartments filled with squally kids, stepping over seaweed drying, dodging halibut strips hanging, nodding to grandmothers sitting in their heat-casemented doors. I felt the sickness without naming the disease (for it was a rich summer, sockeye sold at 18¢ a lb., and plentiful; it wasn't hard times) everytime I walked the longporch out to mend my net or buy a bottle, everytime I walked the longporch home to sit at home and drink and wait for Sady. That may have been the problem: summer's richness didn't end with summer. It was *such* a good season we had food all winter long without having to go jig for cod, and though we had no toilets, we had booze.

Ah, booze! When I recall that summer and the winter following, I get dizzy with headache—a ten-year-old hangover! We had booze. We finished out the summer and though Sady had to take a few days off to get her wrists taped, and I snagged a guy's net setting in the dark one night while drunk and had to pay him damages, and nearly rammed another guy at Idle Point, we finished off with eight to ten thousand dollars between us, no expenses (no tax, the kids were in school on the Government, we had our winter's food up, the boat was paid for by an Indian fisherman's grant, our house was on Reserveland)—more than triple what we'd ever had before! It was what we'd always wanted and I guess we should have taken a trip out—downtown to see the kids, or Sady could have tried to find her father, old Chief Jesse, or maybe go to Hawaii, Fiji, Mexico! We didn't though. Instead, we sat at home and drank, and drank, and drank, and drank, while the circle of our friends swelled to match our heads, and our earnings shrank to match our minds. It was what the old ones used to do: hoard their summer's wealth to squander at the Winter Carnival: only, where they had to save up many years for one week's blast, ours was a potlatch to end potlatches. Our summer never ceased all winter long and, quick as that! spring had passed, we'd not gone spawning nor seaweeding nor even seen the sun except to hold our aching heads and shade our eyes. And then we're back: gutting pinks and chinooks, making midnight sets, roaring down the longporch (no seaweed or halibut to dodge) booze in hand. . . . What happens? The summer's a short one: socks down to 7¢ a lb., pinks 3¢, and fish are scarce. Most guys fail to meet expenses—gas and grub. Summer's hardly started when Blind Channel closes down and, without a warning, autumn, winter's on us.

But by now we've got the habit, we're too soft for hard times, so off the shelf comes last year's stink-eggs, goat, and deer, and down the gullet goes this morning's homebrew—potato-peel mash, salmonberry juice, even Indian rhubarb flavored with orange pop! With Josh's store, of course, we'll never starve; but he can't operate forever on barter. His store stock's dwindling, old North Wind's blowing, our heads are pounding and our guts griping—winter's here.

That was the winter Sady started going to the Doctor's everyday. Not that a lot of others didn't do the same: they'd crowd into "Out-patients"—all of them women, most with children—to complain about whatever new ailment they could concoct (backache mainly), thumb through old magazines, and get a pill. Just as there was a church crowd, so these were the hospital crowd (though some attended both, Letty for instance). Not that there was so much else to do: school for the young kids, basketball for the drop-outs, sex and booze for the men and ladies. Just that Sady'd never been "one of the crowd," not even of the party crowd. I guess that's why I was surprised when she started going with her mother to the Doctor's. I didn't try to stop her, but neither did I take her part when Josh would kid her. He'd say she had "stove-pipe-itis—also called sooty innards, from taking too much firewater." Josh was surprised, and I think saddened too, at Sady's drinking; she'd always been the one he drank pop with when he was on the wagon; then when he fell off—predictable as Christmas, Sports-day, twice a year (and what binges! Josh made up for lost time)— Sady was the one who'd give him hell the mornings after. I think Josh missed those sessions most of all: Sady standing righteous at the castiron, a poker in her hand, hissing "You stuupid!", Josh hang-dog and remorseful at the breakfast table, supporting in both hands a head bigger than the skulls the anthropologists dug up at Blind Man's Bluff.

But it was Old Gideon's verdict I should have pondered. He considered Sady's drinking a sign of the last days, and her trips to the Doctor's "a whoring after heals for more than body, Son. I know. Since I been hid in Jesus, I can see."

Funny how that holy-roller hokum hides its teeth: you think it's got no hold on you, you think you're immunized; then it sinks its teeth like snakebite till you dance, or die. It was about the time Old Gideon took to his bed and commenced prophesying that Nora started visiting a lot. Now, I never did like Nora. She was my wife's mother and had been married to or lived with most every guy in town, including the late Dr. Sharp my father thought so much of. But that's not what bothered me. Nora'd come by after lunch and then they'd both head up the boardwalk.

"Off to see Pill-puncher," Josh remarked wryly one winter afternoon. He was sitting in the store-front, peeking out.

"I suppose," I said.

"Sure," he grinned, "only this Sharp ain't so sharp as the *old* Sharpster; why, for all we know, Sady's only off to see her brother."

"Half-brother," I corrected him.

"Half-brother, hell!" he grinned, picking up an apple and polishing it, "for all you know, *you're* his half-brother, and Sady's his . . ." he bit into his apple, eyes a-twinkle.

"I get your point, Josh," I said, and left him grinning in his dingy little store-front, peeking out at the boardwalk.

It was February 28, ten years ago, I remember it precisely. Gale warnings out; somewhere out in the Pacific, probably within the twelve-mile limit, herring schools gravid with spawn were being swept shoreward. March came roaring in, while we passed-out. We were having a potato-peel brew party, and after the home-brew was all drunk and the crowd gone home, Sady started begging for the bottle of storebought I had put away to celebrate first sighting of the spawn.

"Tomorrow," I said, "spawn's coming tomorrow. Why, Josh has had his sign out a week now."

"Gotta save some back," Josh winked, "to wet the deck."

"Why can't tonight?" she pleaded, "jus' a liddle," and held her hands up, palms facing to indicate how little.

Josh grinned broadly, "That's a little? Why, the herring would miscarry just to get downwind of you! You'd better go to bed and not imperil this year's spawn, let Nature take its course, eh, Kale?" and he held up thumb and forefinger to illustrate. "You know, Sady," he said, "when you and Kale were dancing earlier, it reminded me of one New Year's Eve I was in Vancouver, and couples requesting songs from the band-leader."

Sady yawned. "Give Sady jus' a liddle, Kale, hummm?" I shook my head, "Damn you!" she cried. Then: "Joshua! *you* tell me where it is, you tell me, and . . ." she looked coyly at me ". . . an' lil' Sady'll take brother herringspawning—t'night! Comeon, Josh."

"One couple, they're newlyweds, ask for a tune, so he

plays *Night and Day.* Sady—are you listening, Sady? Another couple, they've been married a few years like you and Kale, Sady—Sady?"

"What about it, Josh, go herring-spawn with lil' Sady? Hummm?"

"So the band-leader, he plays *Now and Then;* finally, this old couple celebrating their golden anniversary—fifty years, Sady, imagine, fifty years! So what do you suppose he plays for them?"

"I don't give a goddamn what he plays!" she screamed and glared at me. "Tomorrow, if he's any friend of yours!" and stalked out of the house and slammed the door.

After a few minutes of silence, I asked, "What did he play, Josh?" Josh looked up at me, then at his watch; it was just passing midnight: "*Yesterday,*" he said, and smiled weakly.

We emptied the ashtrays and gathered up the glasses and other party things, found a partial plate we supposed belonged to Glennie, and generally straightened up. The records—old scratchy 78's—we stacked beside the gramophone, and went to bed.

It must have been two in the morning when the storm hit: windows rattling, trees swaying, lashing rain and hail and I had to jump up out of bed and throw my clothes on, run down to the beach and wrestle with the skiff, launch in heavy surf, row out through six-foot breakers, board and weigh anchor and run for cover behind Carter's breakwater. Of course, Dan and Fereby and Ben were running too, everyone who'd anchored their boats out, so there was quite a jam-up at the keyhole, Moses jogging backward in the wind and towing David, everybody else waiting his turn except Jasper in the *Janet B.* who rushes in and narrowly escapes ramming ol' Mose; I wait my turn and, Christ! If in the lightning-flash I don't see Sady standing on the rocks at the keyhole, standing arms extended and legs braced facing the storm, as far out on the jutty as it runs, naked or nearly so, without a shred of clothing I could see except the shift she had on earlier half-torn, flung back, and flapping in the breeze—black hair swept back and face raised to the storm. Then the sky turned dark again with just the bobbing lights of little boats. . . . I felt like rushing madly to the quay before anyone could see her; but then, they'd all seen her already, and I felt like jogging backward to Japan for very shame. My turn came finally, but by that time she was gone. I slid into the keyhole after Mose and docked the boat, tied fast the *Sady D.* as I never throughout seven years of marriage could its namesake, and avoided the fellows as I half-ran up the wharfhinge and across the bridge and down the boardwalk home. The wind and rain secluded me, but every now and then a bolt of lightning struck and made me shudder to think God himself was watching.

Sady was home, and by time I got there Janet and Jasper, Josh too, the three of them grouped around the table eating stink-eggs (at least, stink-eggs had been eaten and Janet had had some, and Sady), while Sady stood up to the stove stirring a big steamy pot and breaking (just like they were eggs) old records—the 78's we'd danced to earlier—and plopping them in. I watched aghast.

"What in God's name are you doing?"

She turned and looked accusingly at me. "Making brew," she said simply, and went back to breaking records.

"Making *what?*"

"*Brew*," she said, "Mama showed me how. When you haven't got the makings, you smoke rabbit-weed; when I haven't got the mash, I drink this stuff." She prodded with a long spoon the vile-looking liquid: the sound of shattered glass in a tin pot.

"It's something they coat records with," Josh offered, "to keep them. I've heard of it down skid-row; never tried it though. Never was that hard-up, hope I never will be."

Janet laughed, and I could tell she was half-drunk. "Sady'n me's goin' a little Indian tonight, Josh, whyn't you join us?"

"Can't," he said, extracting from his shirt pocket a pack of gum, "on the wagon."

"Yeh, well," Jasper said as he got up, "see you people. An' you come on home, now, Janet—you hear me?"

She shot him a glance of sheer contempt (when he was standing up she was on a level with him, sitting) and dipped her fingers in the stink-eggs. I sat down.

After awhile Sady's brew was ready and Josh and I looked on as the two of them, then Josh watched while the three of us, holding our noses with one hand tipped "bottoms up." It was without doubt the awfullest decoction man or woman ever drank, or God allowed. One cup and I'd surrendered and got up to get the bottle, but the girls only laughed as Josh nodded guiltily toward the trash.

"I couldn't help it, Kale, they got me down." I glared at him. "They woulda' woke old Gideon," he shrugged, "I swear they would."

And so it went, Josh sitting, chewing, watching the two women eat stink-eggs between cupfuls of the blues and rock, me swilling coffee after one cupful of the stuff and running outside to the toilet. One was enough. I started feeling pains and rued the day we'd ever bought those silly records, ever sent off for that stupid mail-order machine; while Sady and Janet, glassy-eyed and ill—but not ill enough, not yet—as though by having consumed its juice they had the frenzied rock-'n-roll *in* them, turned absolutely manic and like mad women possessed—frantic but not sick, not yet—jumped up and started flailing their arms wildly, stomping feet, wah-hooing like they're dancing Indian. . . .

. . . we usher them into the store-room, but instead of

damping them, the cold air turns them on more. Sady's really
dancing now, nearly in a fit, her eyes rolling. . . . Then I realize
there's something wrong: Sady's skin is splotching purple,
they're both swelling at the ankles, wrists, elbows. . . .

"Go get Dr. Sharp," I order Josh.

"N'ssh," Sady hissed, suddenly exhausted and collapsing
to the cold floor, "he's not the man."

"Go get him, Josh!" And while Josh runs off I yell to Janet,
"Watch her!" and rush off another way to get someone else—
I'm not sure who, one of the old women—when in the front
doorway I run smack into Letty!

"Och!" she jumped, "I thought you was a ghost! Jesus tol'
me bring some medicine to Gideon Stone's place, honest He
did!" And as I tried to squeeze past she opened her Bible to
display some withered devil's-club root pressed to death, I
noticed, between *Malachi* and *Matthew* . . . funny the details
one notices. . . . I noticed in that same split-second Letty's wide
eyes widen till the pupils rolled back leaving only the whites
showing—blind-eyes, eyelids fluttering as pointing and starting
to breath heavy, shaping her mouth to slaver, scream, or gag—
she turned my gaze to Sady twisting in a circle on her hands and
knees, retching, steam rising from the cold floor where the
warm vomit and hot blood from her wrists was spurting out.

"Oh, God!" I groaned, and turned to find a tourniquet
when Letty's shrill glass-shatter shriek broke from behind with
paralyzing sharpness, unnerving me so I could scarcely move
or determine which one to move to. I tried to go to Sady but
Letty by this time had dropped her book and clutched my arm
with both hands, shrieking wildly and with eyes rolled back
—"ɛiy-ɛiy-ɛiy-ɛiy-ɛiy-ɛiy-ɛiy-AEEEEEEEyhAAAAAhh—": now *she*
was in convulsions, lost in Pentecost or epileptic seizure, who
knows which; as Janet backed against the wall and Sady,
weakening, collapsed in her own vomit, writhing, retching still

—the dry heaves now—and choking, suffocating in it like she was drowning.

"Let go, Letty, goddamn you, let me go!" But she only clung harder and screamed shriller as, dragging her with me, I went to Sady to lift her and hold her and call her name, Letty screaming, "EEEEEEEyhEEEEEEEEyhEEEEyhAAAAAAhh," like the blackbird of the storm piercing my ear, as Sady gagged and bit her tongue madly and clawed the air, and Janet hid her face and sank with a low moan against the wall, me holding Sady up while treading water trying to unpry the fishhooked hands gripping my arm pulling me away from her, like raven's talons, struggling like a drowning man with a drowned corpse: "Let go, let go, goddamn you, let go, Letty! . . ."

"Letty, what?—is service over? is she . . . everybody gone?"

"We been gone there an' back again, oh, sixteen choruses ago but Doctor says Dean's bleedin' awful bad an' come an' get you. He is too, I seen it, all them devil pokes they give 'im and them wires, he's cryin' out but nobody can hear 'im in that tent-thing; but I heard 'im, honest, an' I pray for him and everybody in the whole wide world to love Jesus more and for nurses and doctors too to have more power workin' on them, even that nurse. . . . Now you wait, Kaleb Stone! I come to get you an' you're not runnin' off without me; set that picture down, that woman's dead an' gone to Jesus, it's Dean that's cryin' now—wait! wait for me!"

Letty

Honest, I real did see that guy, saw somethin' coming closer goin' like this: "You you you youuuuuuuuuuuuuu," *goin'* like and *goin'* like that—it was really *white*—thinkin' it's a ghost, gee, an' I thought it was one touchin' me like when I walked from the old cannery an' got really scared, where that really deep-hill part is, there's a young kindof young ladylike, I thought she was a ghost she had blonde hair so fair, an' I got really scared of her when she come closer an' closer.

"What's wrong? What's wrong? What are you screaming for?"

"Are-you-a-ghost-are-you-a-ghost-are-you-a-ghost?" — I said that an' she started laughin'.

"No, I'm not a ghost, I'm just a really human bein' like you," an' she touched my hand—thought her hand was gonna go right through my hand and we just started laughin' at each other, well, when this one come out at us out of the hospital *goin'* like and *goin'* like that—it was *really* WHITE—thinkin' it's a ghost, gee, an' I thought it was one touchin' me: "Damn you, Letty, shut up! Will you always follow me?" Kaleb said that, shakin' me, an' here I thought it was this big ghost shakin' me so I screamed "EEEEEEEEEEEEEEEEEEE" an' jumped down here under the boardwalk an' he said, "Here's a quarter," an' flipped it an' went on and started talkin' to that ghost at the hospital door an' I saw then it was only Doctor Sharp.

I do believe in ghosts. Honest, one time I was down here

125

lookin' for monies an' I heard the kids when one of them drop-ped money, "Ah, let Letty pick it up, she'll pick it up I know that," and here it was just near me, you know, a dime or a nickel. I didn't make a noise at all. You know when I hear some-body walkin' over me I stop and wait till they go farther then I start again, huntin' for monies peoples drop. But I went and got scared of a guy once, thought he's just a funny man of the ground—maybe you know him, Sam Angel?—I got so scared I just started screamin' under the boardwalk an' people on the road heard me an' they got scared of me. I thought this Sam Angel was justa funny man of the ground, an' here he was lookin' for monies like I was. We just laugh at one another and keep huntin' an I turned down the wharf way and 'member the tide was way down an' I went where it was kindof deep, stones goin' down like, under the red-railin' bridge. And saw somethin' so-o-o shiny, here it was a quarter, an' used two really long sticks to fish it. And found some other—a dime and nickel. And when I started on that big board road, you know, near Daniel Woodfall's house, and when I started comin' this way, found some more: mostly all pennies the kids dropped. And when I got way over this way found another quarter. That's two dollars straight for the hospital, 'cause I really do give all my monies there, an' I pray too. When I go to bed at nights I pray for TB patients first, pray for them to love Jesus more and even pray for nurses and doctors in TB hospitals; then I pray for the old people in this village and all over the whole world for them to love Jesus more in their hearts and minds and I pray for Jesus to make them strong and healthy and for them to believe in Him. Then I pray for sick patients in this hospital and even for nurses and doctors, and for poor and blind children all over the whole world to love Jesus more and believe we're more rich with Him. Then I pray for the Essendale patients, for every buildin' of that Essendale, not just the ward

Letty

Clinic, and all other hospitals I pray for, and for nurses and
doctors to have more powers in workin' on them. Then I pray
for every human bein' all over the whole world: Russians,
Americans, Canadians, Saskatchewans, all over the whole world
to do be more like brothers and sisters, just travel 'round
visitin' each other. Then I pray for sailors out in the deep blue
sea, not just for the grey sailors, I pray for every boat that's
travellin', for persons on them to love Jesus more; an' if they
ever need help, like if their engine's spoiled or somethin', I pray
for them to love Jesus more and pray to Him in Heaven. Then
when I finish prayin' I pray for myself last, an' if there's anybody dyin' or just dead, pray for their body. Jesus tells me pray
as usual. "You pray as usual, Letty, even if the world is wicked
and the body rots, you pray for Indians and other people,
Letty." An' I really do hear Jesus talk to me as clear as ever I
hear Kaleb talkin', only Doctor Sharp I can't hear 'cause he
whispers. Kaleb's askin' Doctor Sharp what can be done, an'
they're talkin' 'bout downtown. Well, if they send Dean downtown I know he won't be happy 'cause I heard him, early, early
when the frost's still on the boardwalk an' he comes out of the
the nurses' residence blinkin'—oh he's drunk all right—an'
that nurse, the one with the red hair, she's in that blue gown
halfway open, standin' in the doorway with her leg leaned
way out so it's touching him, but he can't do nothin', only
blink like a early-mornin' owl.

"Why don't you?" she says. "Try it, Dean. Everything's
different downtown. And I'll see to it you meet lots of girls your
own age." An' he don't answer, only blinks and nearly falls
down, lookin' up at her. "What's there to lose, anyway, hmmm?"
and jiggles her leg sidewise so she wasn't even dressed proper
for *bed*.

An' he said, early, early Sunday morning, when Jesus

127

said to Mary "Touch me not," he said "Fuck you!" and fell off the boardwalk—I heard 'im and I seen 'im—an' that woman look 'round and run back in and slam the door, an' if I hadn't been beneath near where he landed face down in the muck, he wouldof drownded where the sewer from the nurses' residence spills out. That's how I knowed he wouldn't be happy goin' downtown, but I won't say anythin' to them, just watch an' pray. . . .

BOOK THREE

Doctor Sharp

Doctor Sharp

Dean died this morning. Not that there was ever any question he might live. With a dialysis apparatus he might have malingered a week more, but the trip downtown to reach one would have finished him. So he died this morning, here. Already I've prepared the body, the old women have dressed it, the Pentecosts removed to Kaleb's house: already there's a feeling of relief, of ritual, and already I'm seated at my desk with pen and ledger ready to reduce him to a cipher, a statistic, while the Pentecosts convert him to a spirit, a lost soul.

I enter Dean directly under Danny: same year, same surname, nearly the same age, same cause of death, a different cipher; latest in the list of ciphers all, or nearly all, the same. (Last night pumping Eva Harris' stomach the third time: swallowed a month's supply of nerve pills saved up from her daily visits to "Out-Patients"; craving attention.) Ciphers each one different, all the same—except that women never harm their faces, the men do. Number forty-three: "Sept. 13, 1969: Gideon (Dean) Black Stone, 19, suicide/mental depression." I make the entry, envisaging the room, the gloom, the moment of dying . . . black raincoats and brown faces crowding in and pressing round his bed, not eager, not earnest, not intent, merely resigned: an almost complete ring of gathered gloom, hump-backed with doom—not expecting anything of me, not hoping anything for him, not awaiting any death-bed testimonial which, like the age of miracles, they know has passed—just grouped in gloom in blacks and browns waiting the end, breathing. While Lydia, red, white, with purpled fingernails, strides brazenly across to gaze at him, then back to stand beside the basketball-team boys, eighteen, nineteen, twenty year-olds—Lydia in technicolor, truly insatiable. I make my entry, her latest victim's epitaph; what was present this morning I make past. Dean is as dead now as Samson, as Sisera; let Delilah-Jael-Lydia live on! The past is burdensome enough for me, let Lydia worry the future. Today's cipher is sufficient for today.

I ask myself, is it worse here than elsewhere? Or is it just me, not this place at all? Have I just gotten islanded, bushed? Gone Indian, berserk? Or is everybody else in the same boat only their boat's bigger? They don't know it yet, the water's not yet lapping at their doorstep, so they dream on while their luxury-liner slowly, surely sinks and they drown with it. Is it me, this island, or is it civilization, the whole world? Are these Indians only following the great-apes and sea-monsters in an accelerating order of extinction—those close to nature first, those remote from nature last—in which the carnivores' and city-dwellers' time comes when they've eaten all the rest and maimed each other? And if that's so for Dean and Danny—drowning men whom pride or instinct kept from clamoring aboard a sinking ship, whether by walking the ratline or marrying a nurse—what does that make doctors and missionaries, teachers and nurses? Drowning rats deserting the same stinking, sinking ship—the flagship *Civilization?*

Sometime last night between pumping Eva Harris' stomach and preparing Dean's body I dreamed I was on board a huge oceanliner, sightseeing on deck, though there was water all about my ankles, when suddenly I realized the ship was sinking. I tried to loosen a small life preserver. Others spoke of the ship sinking and tried to find lifeboats. All this time the ship was going down. Looking up, I saw a shore—like Nanootkish: inhospitable and marshy, barren-ground—but from the sinking ship it seemed a refuge, so I set out for it, swimming. I tried to grasp the rope connected to the ship's prow, to tow the ship to shore but it weighed thousands of tons and I gave up. I was just reaching the reef when the ship slid underwater and the whirlpool it created sucked me under, back, and down, inexorably and counter-clockwise round and down I spiraled, and wondered vaguely whether I was moving up . . . or down? When an upturned empty lifeboat from the wreck below—it was more buoyant than I—palmed my outstretched hand and I knew the wake had run its course and was carrying me up now, and wondered whether I would reach the surface sooner . . . or later? More slowly now, spinning in an ever-widening arc, I could see that many ships had sunk just off this reef. Some intact still: hulks and wrecks of old ships, large and small, sailboats, rowboats, none like the huge modern steel-hulked ship I had deserted. I tried in passing to examine their ghost-crews, to determine what exactly had gone wrong. A fleeting glance: two slavish faces which, when they spied me, changed from forgetfullness to anguish, as though I'd woken them and made them remember whatever had caused their ruin. But what it was I couldn't determine nor, it seemed, could they. ("The secrets being given out at death . . ." that phrase. . . .) Next, in a large, masted ship (like the old island peoples': Phoenicians, Polynesians) a girl was being beaten by a man. Then re-enacted right before my eyes, as though they were remembering and reliving the nightmare, both were bludgeoned to death by another man. ("The secrets being given out at death you will discover . . ." that same phrase kept recurring.) Turning still, returning, in ever-widening arcs, another sunken ship perched on the reef hove into view. Here I was to watch a dying child—a twin, I saw, discarded—whose mother sat apart holding the other child, a male, at some festivity, a feast or dance, with a man curiously resembling my father (though his back was turned and I was sure he was a stranger) watching the dance with her, unconcerned. Angry and jealous, I tried to take the child to its mother, though she didn't want it and would let it die, so I could satisfy myself it was not my father with her. But when I saw him, saw for certain it *was* him, I was too choked with passion to draw breath or break the surface, too *involved.* And there on that ship sunk so recently it was still on the reef, I too became one of the drowning. . . . ("The secrets being given out at death you will discover are not worth waiting for."—letter from my father, the year before he died.)

I knew on waking that the sunken ships were civilizations; but more important to me was the image of my father, and the myth of the discarded twin. It was a myth, I knew, because I'd checked it out on my trip downtown—hunting up Lila Brampton Marsh, R.N. (still Miss, still Matron at the Coquilitza Residential School though ready to retire and write her memoirs, tell "her story" to whomever would sit still and listen and "Don't interrupt, so long as you don't interrupt I don't mind telling you, since you're his son and a son's entitled, especially a first son—are you a first son?" "No, a second." "Well, a son's entitled to know what there is to know about his sire and your father was a fine man, I only met your mother once and that was after Dr. Sharp had gone to glory, but your father . . ."), sitting in the small but comfortable attic flat connected to the clinic which was connected to the dorm where native children ages five to eighteen from every village on the coast were sent at the discretion of the Indian Agent or the Public Health Nurse to live and learn to walk the ratline, walk on water, sitting patiently watching the bunned hair bob with emphasis (I wondered vaguely whether Lydia's was dyed too), listening quietly to the long story which was of some but not exceeding interest, being mainly about *her*, until she reached in strict chronological sequence the three or four years she was stationed at Nanootkish.

"There wasn't any hospital there then, no school to speak

of either. You see, I came in 1939. Your father had been there how many years already? Fifteen or twenty, anyway—a one-man missionary, doctor, teacher, magistrate, postmaster, linch-pin so to speak with the outside world, with civilization! The schedule that man kept! Anyway, I arrived in 1939, I left in 1943; you remember the war-years?"

"Vaguely," I replied, "sugar rationing and such."

"Well, we fought a little war there of our own. It was civilization versus savagery, just like against the Nazis, only the savagery in this case was all centered at the air-base, and the civilizing factor was your father."

"I've heard there was an air-base," I began, "at Whiskey Sluice, but from the air you'd never know it now."

"One hardly knew it then," she said, "what with camou-flaging, black-outs, lookout posts in every tree-top—they were so afraid of air-raids, so afraid, and not a single plane was spotted the whole time! Anyway, there were twelve hundred men there, just across the straits, in need of hospital facilities, religious services, and rules—a doctor and a chaplain and a judge—and who thought they needed, as they called it, 'sex and booze'. Their true needs your father saw to; the village saw to the other. It was an awful time, I tell you, and that man-of-God. . . ." Her voice wavered with emotion, remembering no doubt some episode in which, safely aligned with light, she'd witnessed darkness and liked it. ". . . Why, I remember him ringing the nurses' residence doorbell one night, it must have been three or four a.m. The village was off-limits, the whole village, and blacked-out, but nurses and teachers could invite the airmen over. He rang and rang till he woke the whole house up: 'Why, whatever do you want?' we asked him. 'It's past midnight, Dr. Sharp.'

" 'It is indeed,' he said, 'and I want that boy out.'

" 'What boy?' we asked, and the four or five of us there looked at one another. 'What boy, Dr. Sharp?'

We, the Wilderness

" 'That boy that's in bed with Patsy Cline,' he said, 'I want him out right now, and I want his name and rank and serial number tomorrow.' Then he stalked away and, sure enough, there was an airman hiding under Patsy's bed—who would have guessed?—and your father dismissed her the next morning and married them that same afternoon.

"Oh, he was sharp!" she laughed. I smiled politely. "What I mean is, nothing passed him by. He patrolled that village every night and it blacked-out and everyone, or most everyone, in bed and asleep by five p.m. in wintertime. Your father made the rounds at five o'clock, nine o'clock, and midnight, and he was up and working everyday by six. Oh, towards the end girls starting rowing to Grave Island after dark, and Jesse Blackstock's house—you know, next to the hospital?—remained the den of iniquity it always had been. Oh, how I pitied that poor Hilda!"

"The name's familiar," I said.

"She was a lovely girl, the loveliest young girl in the village."

(Sept. 19, 1958: Died Hilda Marie Blackstock, 35.)

"The loveliest native girl I've ever seen, with long black hair, fine features. . . ."

(—suicide/slashed wrists, R.S.)

". . . with that ogre for a father, oh, he was chief then but he'd do *anything* to keep himself in liquor. Why, nearly every morning from the hospital window we'd watch the boats load he'd had there all night, rowing their drunken way across the straits, and after a year or two you never did see Hilda, she was confined, imprisoned in her room. And you never attended any big 'do' in the village—beer bingo, whiskey social, or what not—but what Jesse was toastmaster.

" 'On behalf of the men I'd like to say, on behalf of the village, will the parents *please* on behalf of the players keep their childrens off the floor!' Behalfing this, and behalfing that, the more liquored up he got the more behalfs! And that poor Hilda, then her younger sister Wilma—lucky for Sady and Janet they were married by that time—home alone tied to the bedposts. It was awful! And your poor father going there two, three times weekly to stop it."

"What did the mother say?" I asked.

"Nora? She condoned it. From all I gather she was too liquored up herself to say boo; anyway, Jesse would have hit her if she had."

"He was that bad, was he?" I asked, contrasting her report with old Willie's peaceable account.

"Worse. Jesse Blackstock was a savage, a real beast. Oh, he was likeable enough when sober—like Crow, his half-brother —but self-important, surly, snarly, that's when he was drink-ing, and thanks to Hilda and the war he nearly always was. That, at least, is what your father said, and he should know; he had to put up with him. Yet I will say this for Jesse: he was always civil and polite to me. In fact, I always found it difficult to countenance the stories of what went on at his place, until one night I saw it for myself." She stopped and looked at me, eyes glowing, gleaming with a voyeur's delight to re-experience what once she'd witnessed and for two-score barren years since had cherished. On the basis of that look alone I adjudged Miss Lila Brampton Marsh to be a venal, not a vestal, voyeur.

"You witnessed it yourself," I prompted.

"Did I! Jesse was asleep when I came searching for your father; I could see him through the broken pane in the side door, snoring on the kitchen floor passed-out, with dice and cards, cigar butts and old bottles on the table, and a sink and counter full of greasy dishes and leftovers. I tiptoed past and heard through the partition (it wasn't in the front room, but that little closet-bedroom off the front room, the one where Hilda's grandmother, they say, lay twenty years clawing the wallpaper off the four walls, scrap by scrap). I heard the muffled cries and raucous laughter, shuffling and stumbling, thudding, falling—slithery, I tell you!—and heard Jesse snoring on the floor behind me, so I stepped on in the front room (Wilma must have been asleep upstairs, and Nora) and there in lantern light (the door into the little room was cracked a bit so that light penciled out to where I stood peering, yes, I was peering in) there was Hilda in that windowless bedroom, you know the one that faces west, bound wrists and ankles to the bedposts, being. . . ." She stopped rocking and leaned forward and her voice sank to a low passionate whisper, "Doctor, there were four men on her, four, and. . . ." She shut her eyes and paused. "She couldn't cry for help but her eyes were open through it all, staring straight up at the ceiling at, I suppose, the scraps of wallpaper her grandmother had left, or maybe seeing Jesus, I don't know, but staring straight up with the rapt gaze of a saint, God *bless* her!"

Rest her, I corrected quietly.

"And then she choked, she choked on that foul, evil thing! And Jesse came up behind me, well-liquored you could tell, both in the way he said it and the words he used: 'On behalf of the girl, Miss Marsh, and on behalf of her poor mother, on behalf I say of all concerned and 'specially on behalf of me and Doctor Sharp who isn't here, maybe you're looking for him, but. . . .' 'In the Name of God! Jesse,' I cried, and started backing towards the front door. '. . . on behalf of Him too, Miss Marsh, I ask you, don't go in there.' And I was out the front door and down the boardwalk and back home before he begged on anybody else's 'behalf of'!" She shook her head and the orange bun at the back bobbed like a metronome.

"Those were bad years for Nanootkish, the war years, but I've never had a more memorable placement." She leaned back and commenced rocking again, a little flushed.

"Tell me," I said, after what seemed an appropriate silence, "do you recall a baby born to Nora, a stillbirth?"

"Oh yes, it was just about the time old Jesse died."

"Or disappeared," I said.

"Or disappeared," she smiled. "As I remember, I signed the delivery papers, though I wasn't there the whole time."

"You weren't there?"

"No."

"But you signed the papers?"

"I was there for the delivery of the stillbirth, not the other."

"The twin?" I said.

"That's right. I signed for the stillbirth; but there was intervening labor, no complications that I know of, so your father relieved me and stayed to deliver the other. He signed for it himself."

"Oh, yes," I said. "Do you recall, was that a boy or a girl?"

"A boy, I think. You'll find it in the register, I'm sure."

"Right. One thing more, I know it's hard to remember after all these years, but I have this application to fill out and some of the records have been misplaced, it's easier to ask you than hunt for them. Do you recall, by any chance, whether or not Nora's baby, the stillbirth, was Indian? I mean, of full Indian parentage?"

She peered at me quizzically, much as she must have peered at Sodom and Gomorrah through the cracked door. "The problem is," I said, "whether or not this boy, the other one, the twin, is to be granted the Indian rights he's applied for." I waited.

"No," she said searchingly, "no, I don't think they were. At least, the stillbirth wasn't."

"So unless the Indians' theory about twins is right, that they've two different fathers. . . ."

"And genetic theory wrong."

"Right. It's unlikely that the other one was either. Well,"

We, the Wilderness

I said cheerily, rising from my chair, "we'll just have to put the truth down on that application, won't we? Let the chips fall where they may."

"The truth never hurt anyone, Doctor," she said, shaking my hand at the door, "I've lived by that these fif—well, many years." She patted her dyed hair, a little flustered. "A woman may feel younger than she looks," she said and smiled. We both smiled. As I left her apartment I had the curious suspicion she'd been telling half-truths all along.

But who was there to go to? Hilda was dead, Sady was dead, now Danny and Dean—all Nora's children and all dead by their own hand. Nora dead too. Jesse Blackstock, the reputed father, missing. Who was there to ask?

My father was, as Miss Marsh put it, "gone to glory," and Nora, if half of what I'd heard of her was true, was gone to grief. Whatever they'd gone to, both the principals were missing, which left as possible informants Jesse Blackstock, still in hiding, and unlikeliest of all, my own mother! Increasingly I had a sense of having to conjure the dead as I searched the produce stands downtown for signs of Jesse Blackstock, and visited my mother at her home.

She still lived in the "summer home" my father built for her where, except for a few years in Nanootkish as a newlywed and an around-the-world cruise as a new widow, she'd spent her whole life. And since it stood on the same site as the house she was born in, chances are she would have lived there whether or not she had married my father. A large clapboard house with many windows, many flowers in the front, and a large garden at the rear; a lattice-work verandah with a swing in the backyard, and a tiny one-room hut set further back. This last my father added to relieve my mother of providing hospitality to countless natives "stuck" downtown visiting sick relatives, hunting winter work, taking upgrading courses. In practice she was doubly relieved, because as often as they lodged there she employed them as "help," so she almost always had "a man" to do the yard and work her garden, and "a girl" to keep the house and do her laundry and cooking. One such "girl," sixty or sixty-five years old, practically raised my brother and me. This was as near the "Indian work" as my mother ever wished to be. And in case I had forgotten she reminded me anew, sitting brittle as a winter flower stalk in the gazebo my father had built especially for her african violets, sitting straight and white and waspish in that many-windowed room while winter sunlight cast a pale light over her, a sourceless and diffuse light not quite warming, warning me with upraised finger not to get involved "in all that Indian work. It's foolish Roger, why, they're dying anyway, aren't they? Isn't that the gist of what you're saying? Why deprive yourself? Why drive yourself to death? 'Because father did,' " she mimicked, " 'and he was a great man, Mother'. Well, he's dead now, and where am I? Where does that leave me? Well, where?"

"You're provided for, Mother."

"Provided for! To travel by myself around the world—you think that's fun? Try it. With two old ladies talking your ear off! Yes, I mean Miss Flora Armitage and Lily Peter. I have to think of things to occupy myself; it's not easy—volunteer work, Prodeo Club, hand work; of course I have my plants, but I run out. Don't tell me I should read and meditate, either; I spend lots of time in secret, Roger, lots! You're away up there, and Chester, though he's in the city, hardly ever comes by, but I understand," she waved wearily, "he has his family. What I mean, dear, is your father should be with me now, he could be travelling with me, we could be seeing things, enjoying things, together. But no, instead he stayed up there, depriving me and driving, always driving himself, why he drove himself to death! It was inconsiderate, Roger. And why? All for those Indians who are just dying anyway, you can't stop them, Roger, you might as well not even try."

"Mother." But she'd lapsed into pouting, and no amount of coaxing could cajole her until we walked out back to the little verandah and felt pale winter sunshine dry and brittle on our necks; and while she watched me from the swing behind the latticework I took the spade and turned some leaf-mold and frost-bitten stalks of flowers. After awhile I came and sat beside her and said: "Mother, I've been thinking. . . ."

"Since old Eben Sandy left hospital that last time, I haven't had a proper gardener," she mused.

"I've been thinking, Mother, about getting married." I thought that was the best way to broach it. "But before. . . ."

She turned on the swing and eyed me thoughtfully. "It's been my great grief," she said, "never to have had a daughter. I suppose this means I'll no longer have a son."

"On the contrary, Mother. I should think. . . ."

" 'A son is a son till he takes him a wife; a daughter's a daughter all the days of her life.' Chester's wife has her own people, and I suppose your girl will too."

"That's what I wanted to talk to you about, Mother," I said.

Her eyes narrowed. "Who is she?" Then, "Not one of those Indians, I hope! Ro-ger. . . ."

"No, no, Mother," I said, patting her, "there's no one. I've just been thinking maybe I *ought* to be married, and. . . ."

"What chance have you to meet a nice girl way up there?"

"There are nice Indian girls," I said.

"Ro-ger," she pronounced with syllabic precision, "there are, I am sure, nice Indian girls, and there are nice Indian boys they can marry. But when any Indian girl, nice or otherwise, so turns *your* head that you consider marrying her, then you've been in that place long enough, *too* long, I'd say—you're depriving yourself, Roger, just like your father!"

"Father was in Nanootkish how many years, Mother?"

"He was deprived."

"But he was married."

"Your father may have had washmaids, one-night companions—that indeed was one of the ways in which he was deprived—but he never mentioned one by name or brought one here. Why, he wouldn't be seen in the company of Indians downtown, much less get addled over one! No, Roger, your father had more sense than that, and I hope you do."

"He never mentioned any one by name?" I probed.

"No! He cer-tain-ly did not!"

And there we left it: me promising her I would, as she put it, "keep my skirts clean," and consider leaving Nanootkish the coming spring; her calling me "her baby, the one she worried about," while assuring me that my father, in whose footsteps I had followed, was nonetheless "a kind and a good man."

"Even though he deprived himself, Mother?"

"And me," she said, "he deprived me too."

Locating Jesse Blackstock wasn't really necessary anymore. The basic fact was known: my father *had* had village women, had in all probability had children by them; only the specifics were wanting. The specific ratio between Cain's deed and Onan's seed, between the blood and sperm spilled out on the ground and in the body—how much stuck? how many?—on the rain-leeched rocky barrenground *WidsWilse* . . . in the dark warm nubile underbelly of *Peacemaker*. Not that Jesse Blackstock, first man out, would know who or how many came after, but he might know why; he might even see my father as the victim, surrounded and absorbed by the dark womb of the village as the village was surrounded by the sea. He might. But then again, he might be bitter, vengeful . . . or dead.

Going from Willie's story, I had been looking for a swart, prosperous truck-farmer with a late model pick-up and a white wife. Now I started inquiring after an abdicated Indian chief and, going by Letty's story, asked first at Essendale. Oh, yes, "The Chief," they called him, lived an hour's drive from there with a daughter (the attendant, a young man, rolled his eyes suggestively and grinned broadly). Periodically this "Chief" went berserk while on a binge and had to be committed. But he raised a few root crops which, to encourage him, the hospital had contracted to buy on a cash basis; delivery, the attendant said, was never prompt.

I followed the directions given me by the attendant, driving my mother's new, low bucket-seater over two or three gullied sideroads and wondering, as the farms and open fields got scarcer, what sort of place, what sort of person I was looking for. Would I be surprised when I got there and found him, would I be sorry I had come?

The fields and farms gave way to rocky, rain-leeched holdings in among foothills. Deserted or dismantled barns and one- or two-room cabins, smokeless, were spotted among the scrub-pine. The road turned now into a gouged and gullied scar, no fields, no farms, no fence on either side, only bare clay banks and scrubby pine, cedar, and hemlock, with now and then a little clearing in the woods and a ravine across the road I'd bounce through and scrape over. I slowed, coming to the end of the concession. Half a mile or so back, I'd missed the turn. Backing up until I'd found the entryway, I turned the car around and got out, climbed over the clay bank, and there it was: an unpainted weather-grey shack, slouched back against dense trees with stumps in front and a little cleared ground, maybe half an acre, to the side. An ancient pick-up truck, on blocks, sat near the plowed ground, an old plow-horse near a shed to house him in and, in the middle of the plowed ground, a man, Indian, squatting by a massive cedar stump smoking a pipe. All this a hundred yards away so that, except for the smoke from the man's pipe, and the smoke from the shack's stovepipe, I would never have noticed man or shack; and except for the flies—it was a grey, dull, sluggish day; late afternoon—and the rhythmic tail-swishing, I would never have noticed the horse either. They noticed me of course, of that I'm sure; nothing changed though, no one moved, until I started walking toward the man.

When I got to within fifteen or twenty paces of him, he blinked both eyes, froglike; he never moved though, never quit smoking. Without removing from his mouth the crook-stemmed pipe, he yelled toward the shack, "Hilda, Heel-dah!" then shifted his squat weight and thrust his hand out. "Twenty bucks," he said, regarding at knee-level my approach. He was a hawk-nosed, yellow-eyed old Blackstock, heavily built and deadpan as the plowshare at his feet.

"Twenty . . .?" I repeated quizzically. He eyed me with contempt, drew back his hand, withdrew his pipe.

"It's not much," he said grimly, "she's not much," and spit towards the shack where, leaning in the open doorway, Hilda watched. For an instant I thought she was Sady, but prettier, prettier but thinner, much thinner and more wasted, wasted in a bright, consumptive way . . . the way she leaned her weight, her weightlessness, against the doorjamb, the way she seemed to meld into the weathered wood and dense bush beyond, the way she seemed to draw you to her with that fervid gaze. . . . The eyes reminded me of Nora, only brighter, deeper; but the weightless body was her mother's, was Hilda's (the Hilda who had spent the war bound to a bed, staring upwards with the rapt gaze of a saint at the scraps of wallpaper her grandmother had left, then slashed her wrists). . . . This Hilda, her daughter, my half-sister maybe, signalled without sound or sign, without need or recognition, across the dull dead grey flat black-fly afternoon that suicidal rapture, that same fever! From that I knew that more than terminal TB ravaged her body. For the same mad urgency to consume and be consumed pounded *my* temples, and I was none of Nora's, and Hilda was none of my pale mother's, and we neither maybe, though separately dammed, were any of the alcoholic abdicated chief's who squatted, hand out-thrust, demanding toll.

What happened was Hilda disappeared inside the shack, Jesse Blackstock put his hand out, I pulled my wallet out and took out twenty to give him, then crossed the red clay rain-mired ground as if this was the field of blood, and entered the shack sweating, swatting black-flies on my neck. She was coughing: lying face down on a cot, her mouth pressed in a pillow. Her dark hair wasn't black, her flushed skin wasn't brown; she was half-white.

"Hilda," I said, sitting on the cotside, and patted her back briskly to stop her coughing. "Hilda." She turned her face toward the wall and as inconspicuously as possible I passed my handkerchief to her. When she was finished, she turned to face me.

"Don't," she whispered hoarsely, "for your own sake. I'll get your money back."

I waved my hand vaguely to indicate it didn't matter.

"Don't kiss me then," she pleaded, "just please don't kiss." Her eyes were bright and feverish, compelling; her face and, as she started unbuttoning her blouse, her neck were flushed.

"No, no," I said, and lay my hand on her hand to stop her and, as I did, felt a great Hand—something I had never felt before—press my head down. My hand was gripping her hand while my face thrust in her neck, inflamed and flushed; now I was groping blindly in her blouse and kissing, searching wildly for her mouth as she struggled vainly against me, as she clenched her teeth and fiercely shook her head until pinned and spent, she lay still while I kissed her on the mouth, and kissed and kissed her mouth until she doubled up coughing and turned onto her side against the wall.

146

When the seizure was over and she'd spit blood again, she raised up on her elbows to face me. "Why, why did you do that?" Her eyes were bright, intense. I shrugged sincerely. After studying me with that same fervent fever-stare, she slumped down onto the bed. "Who are you, anyway?" she said, gazing absently at the ceiling.

"Your brother," I said.

"You're not Danny," she said, matter-of-factly.

"No."

"You're that doctor, aren't you? *His* son."

"Yes," I said.

She turned to look at me with what *I'd* call the rapt gaze of a saint, if there were any, and pressing my hand she whispered, "Do you know the Lord's Prayer?"

I nodded.

"Please," she said.

II

The seineboat flanked by gill-netters proceeds against stiff wind across the straits. Spray; scud; wet sun and sudden sleet. The men and pallbearers, black ribbons flying from their shoulders, stand braced on the flat table stern where, summers, the net lies. The women veiled and dressed in black are huddled round the coffin amidships, over the hold; older women and children are crowded forward in the cabin. I sit on the lee gunwale, dodging spray.

Midway up our mainmast a black flag whips. Black pennants flap from the two gill-netters' stabilizer poles, but ours the flagship, ours the coffin-bearer, ours the *Q. Kilbella;* flanking us the *Sady D.* and the *Janet Lee.* Kaleb, Hazen and Laverne, Josh, Dan, and thirty others, thirty-odd others on the same flagship including Letty, Pastor Moses, Deacon Harper, Rector Bell, and I, have hoisted our colors, have left behind the village of

147

waiting for the island of dying, have set out in dead earnest for Grave Island. At least two of us on this boat have—Dean and me.

On either side of Dean the black flag bearers: children. They're cold, but is he colder? Will the food the old women brought warm him? Will the fire they light to burn his food and possessions placate him, or only them? Is the grave cold as this ocean spray? Remembering the seepage on Grave Island at high tide, I get up and go inside the cabin where it's warm.

Crowded on benches around the bolted-down table by the stove are a dozen old matriarchs with eight or ten children standing or squeezed in. Old Phereba motions to one of her great-granddaughters to move over and I sit down on the food locker where Laurie was sitting, but there's not room for both of us so she stands up. I offer her my knee; she blushes, hides her face; old Phereba says *"Ahayani"* (*uncle, brother*) and fiercely motions her to sit. She sits, rigidly at first, gradually relaxing as the boat rocks and I catch her, gradually she settles in my lap.

She is ten, maybe eleven, very soft yet firm, quite lovely. I have seen her body annually, every year for ten: the clean, uninterrupted straight-line of it, two quick slits—one vertical, one horizontal—smooth, intact, pre-pubic, not even nascent hair . . . the nervous trust of virgin wilderness, ungun-shy still. . . . But why should she be gun-shy? She is with her *Ahayani*, Doctor Sharp, who has often caught himself gazing out of the hospital window, watching her play on the board-walk lithe and graceful as a young doe. She has lovely deep brown eyes too, glistening black hair, an oval face with childish dimples, and a small pouty mouth. The only thing not beautiful about her are her teeth, but she has developed an intriguing way of smiling with her eyes and lips and dimples, without opening her mouth. She turns and smiles at me and, smiling back, I run my tongue over my teeth, conscious of the tartar, plaque, and nicotine stains coating them.

They are launching the last skiff now to go ashore. Laurie looks at me and smiles that enigmatic smile before jumping down and leading me to the siderail to board. There are only a few old women left, the skipper Ben, Laurie and I. One of the basketball team rows us, the last skiffload. Dean and the pallbearers and the two preachers went first; they and all the rest are at the graveside now, waiting. . . .

We jump out on the gravel beach and enter trees, hushed, dark, where dancing shafts of sunlight dapple damp moss-mounded ground; no breeze at all here, only arrows of sunlight through tree-tops piercing mounds and markers, broken shards of pottery, deer-fern, and totem-poles. A somber village of the dead. In spots where sunlight lingers, steam rises from wet sphagnum.

Laurie takes my hand and leads me to the graveside circle where within a cluster of fresh hummocks, close-packed as children sleeping under blankets in a bed and all unmarked (except by short black flags, a veritable forest of black flags: these are those not dead a year yet, not yet named), a fresh wet mound of gravel and a grave-hole, two black flags; deep in the cavity Dean is enboxed as in a boat without a rudder, without chart or compass, without port or destination—a boat moved by the moon and tidal seepage. Laurie peers but is too short to see inside; as far as she can see the hole is empty, bottomless. She focuses a moment on the black flags, on the sunlight dancing on the ground, the nearby tree-trunks, totem-poles, the tree-tops swaying, smiling; smiling without opening her mouth she tugs my hand to see: a V of trumpeter swans brightly overhead, their trumpeting blown southward before them. . . .

I am the resurrection and the life, whosoever . . . her attention is caught briefly until she spots the source, old Bell reading from a book. As well Bell singing, "I want a gur-rul, just like the girl. . . ." Married for twelve years to Nanootkish. Death do thee part. Congratulations, Roger. Father married to Nanootkish forty years. How many gur-ruls? Laurie smiling secretly, in colloquy with swans. . . .

. . . inasmuch as this our brother here departed . . . her head cocked slightly, studying a totem, wolf-totem of the Blackstock clan. How many brothers here departed? Half-brothers, sisters too. Forty-two (Danny), forty-three (Dean), too many and too far, this has gone too far. . . . How many wolves?

. . . inasmuch as this our brother here departed . . .

earth to earth (plahpt!), in the sure and certain hope . . . Slowly and demurely she uncocks her head, her braided hair falls loose, revealing what? The dark patch darker than blind darkness? The birthmark blacker than brown skin, than blood? "All who worship what is not real knowledge, enter into blind darkness; those who delight in real knowledge, enter into greater darkness." (Letter from my father just before he died.) "All who worship what is not the true cause, enter into blind darkness; those who delight in the true cause, enter into greater darkness." Without glancing at me, Laurie takes my hand, her loosened hair falls down over her neck; without a word she leads me from the circle of mourners . . .

. . . before the silver cord is snapped, or the golden bowl is broken, or the pitcher is broken at the fountain, or the wheel broken at the cistern . . . slowly and demurely and aware precisely of the gentle secret she has shown me, leads me over tree-roots and around fresh water, water seeping over tree-roots, dripping down rock-moss, pure clear fresh deepspring water runneling to sea . . .

. . . and the dust returns to the earth as it was, and the spirit returns to God who gave it. Vanity. . . . along a woodspath to the far side of Grave Island where only old, old graves, or no graves are. . . .

"Laurie . . . Laurie." We are playing a game now. She crouches down behind a pile of bleached clamshells, hides her eyes, while I hide shells she has selected—in a massive upturned tree-root, in its canted crotch, one in a nearby fern-clump, one behind a granite marker. Then I call her, "Laurie." She comes smiling, scanning the grounds quickly while I hold up four fingers. Immediately she runs to the great root and holds up the first shell, pivoting in a half-turn as she does so, pouting slightly —there! She points to the crotch and as I lift her clasps the treasure, hops nimbly down in perfect cadence searching trees, ground, grave—there! Stoops behind the granite marker, pausing delicately, poised in mid-motion, in mid-dance, a slight frown furrowing her brow.

"What's that?" she asks, and points to the giant table-rock laid bare when the great tree which had grown over it was uprooted in a storm. I come and look: carved in the rock a shallow basin-like depression and another, nearly square design with various imprints and center-ridge for, Willie told me once, breaking copper.

"This must have been the long house floor where people lived once," I replied.

Laurie studied it awhile. "What people?"

"The people who ate those," I said and nodded toward the clams, "and those," a second clam-mound.

"Those too?" she asked, discovering a third hillock of clamshells. The ancient mounds, though large, were only the late peaks of a buried mountain of clamshells; the entire north end of the island where we stood, twenty or thirty feet above tide-line, owed its flatness to a clamshell base and single giant rock.

"Those too," I said. She gazed at me almost in disbelief. "Lots of people lived here," I told her, "a long time."

"Not at Nanootkish?"

"No," I said, remembering that the first missionary (before

my father even, before time) threatened a TB epidemic unless the villagers moved from Old Town where they'd always lived, a salmon spawning grounds, to the present site of Nanootkish where TB ravaged them. "Not Nanootkish."

"Not at Blind Channel either," she insisted, "at the cannery?"

"No," I said again, picturing the fetid sink-hole of crowded army barracks without toilets, "not Blind Channel either. Someplace like this, or like Old Town, where there was food, and tall trees, and copper floated in from big boats sunk out in the ocean—Spanish boats and Portuguese and English, Dutch and German, Russian boats," I said, carried away by the geography lesson. "See, here's where the old chief sat and broke copper." I picked up a piece of loose bark and placed it on the square over the center-ridge and broke it; Laurie looked on idly.

"Look!" she cried and ran to the far end of the flat rock, a good seventy or eighty feet distant, where its jagged prow precipitated straight down to the sea, "this must be where they danced when they were happy! And here!" making a half-turn, her half-braided hair outphlanged, "here's where they cooked and ate their dinner—clam chowder," she laughed, "and the children slept—here!"

"Must be," I said, watching her skip lightly over the old surface, scattering handfuls of clamshells.

Then rushing up to me, "Sit there," she ordered and seating me in the chief's place she uprooted some deer-fern and laid it in the basin. "While dinner's on," she said, "I'll dance for you—Grannie showed me how," she blushed. "Here, you beat time with this stick, but first help me with my braids."

And, following instructions, I finished unbraiding her black hair, discovering anew and tingling to unveil the dark patch darker than dark skin, the melancholy black birthmark splayed upward on her neck. Already, as I parted and unbraided the rich hair, already I had come to cherish it.

Doctor Sharp

While I beat time she danced, her nearly nubile limbs vibrant in the sea-breeze, her rich black hair unhindered, loose and free. So natural it seemed, her dancing there on the great rock, an entire ocean at her back, a whole people underfoot; so natural and with such seeming ease. I scrambled up and to her inexpressible delight tried dancing with her, touching at arms' length her fingertips while shuffling to the rhythm I imagined I could hear. It was a game, our game, and when through trees I spied the two gill-netters half across the straits, then, rounding the point, the seine-boat—not searching, not tacking close (probably each thought we'd boarded the other), instead of running to the beach to signal them, I clasped her hand in mine and pointed.

"They're going home," I said.

"They're leaving us?"

"Probably they don't know we're here."

"Nobody knows we're here," she said looking at me, then at the tall trees grown spectral in grey mist. She shivered slightly, then pressed her little body close to mine. "I'm not afraid," she whispered, "not at all."

It was near dusk when finally we found the mausoleum, tripping over rusty sewing machines and getting tangled in old bedsprings and other unidentifiable debris from former burnings, former debacles from former days; dusk, and the mausoleum was right down at the tide-line on a bare rock promontory with a few surrounding gravestones anchored in the crevices of tide-washed rock and tangle of seaweed and wire from artificial wreaths.

Here, of course, was where my father was buried, though like the Indian graves it had been broken into, by curio-hunters and anthropologists, and like all island graves it had been so battered by high-tide that the heavy wooden door, about four feet high, was hinged still but ajar. On top of the stone house a wealth of flora had sprung up in the foot-deep moss and lichen that had somehow taken root. Peering inside by the light of a match I was relieved to see a blanket of lush moss aspread the coffins and old boards, some of them plundered and unpiled, but all moss-covered.

"Laurie," but she was right behind me. "This is where we'll stay the night, Laurie, are you afraid?"

"No," she whispered, then: "Is it a house?"

"It is a house," I answered in a whisper—her awe now, like her energy earlier, I found infectious, "a grave-house, where. . . ."

"Shhh," she whispered, pressing my hand tightly, "we might wake them!"

Swinging wide the door I stooped and crept inside, Laurie in hand. The match burned down and burned my fingers, I dropped it and was surprised to see it flare for a moment. I lit another before feeling for a spot and squatting down. Laurie stood beside me, peering at the tiers of coffins, three and four high, only partially concealed I saw now by the moss which rooted where the top biers had been broken into. The moss seeped out and down along the coffins, sucking nourishment from every crack and worm-hole it encountered, then carpeted thinly across the floor to where she stood and involuntarily shivered and shrunk near me. "We'll build a fire," I said, and was surprised to say it; it wasn't something I had planned to do, but then neither had I planned that dance with Laurie at the long-house. "Here, hold this while I gather up some wood." And while Laurie held the flickering match and discarded and lit one after another, I dismantled the sideboards of two old rotten coffins and piled them just outside the open door with moss and dry-rot kindling beneath.

In no time we had a small fire going, with the mausoleum and the whole of Grave Island between it and the village, so there was little possibility of being seen. Not that the village would have missed us anyway, as yet: no one would miss me unless an emergency came up, and Laurie like most of the children in the village had half-a-dozen homes—aunts and uncles, parents, grandparents, and greatgranny—each of whom would conjecture she was with another, as the boats had, none of whom would miss her overnight.

In a way I was sorry she had come along. Her presence had confused an issue which had seemed clear-cut. If my father had, for good or ill, tyrannized the village; if he had made the Indians dependent upon him, so much that the children of the people he subjected demanded the same from his successor—who else?—the second Doctor Sharp, his son; and if I wouldn't, couldn't do that, if it made me sick inside, and if their feeling of betrayal was so great that forty-three of them committed suicide (Lydia, of course, could count coup too, with her grandfather, Bishop Sommers), why, then, the solution was simple: join them. Be one of the betrayed, rather than betrayer. Be victim, rather than victimizer. Better a dead doctor than a guilty dog.

But Laurie, sitting in the circle of the fire, her head thrown back, was steadily undermining my resolve. The cinders off the old wood rose in a spiral, as she mused with that gentle quiet smile, warm now, about death and life and old people . . .: Did animals die too? Did people become animals after they died? Letty said the ones that drowned did, did they really? Was there really an otter-man who used to be a person, who fed dead people on Grave Island, fed them children? Musing with that enigmatic smile, chin uptilted and throat bared, firelight dancing on her neck and upturned face, she gazed up at stars where no stars were. Her mere pensive presence now (as, earlier, her enthusiasm) was weakening my determination.

Not that I couldn't do what I'd set out to do, only now there was a witness; more than witness, a cajoler inviting me to witness and delight in all things equally as she did—the fire, the sea, the rock on which we sat; in spectral trees and things imaginary; stars where no stars were; in animals half-human; corpses likely to be wakened; in all things quick and sleeping, undying, ever-shifting, all commingled in one child's-eye view of mystic wilderness which, whatever else might happen (and what could, really?) would endure. It was, she was, a sight most disconcerting, who, when I tried to shrink back in the mausoleum, drew me out—with questions, requests to braid, unbraid her hair, more questions, then snuggling close to me in such a sleepy and warm way, so intimately yielding and dependent and self-sure, trusting so, I knew I must that instant embrace her and all creation, All: the Quick and the Dead and the Not-Yet— fillip my Father!—for all things WERE! and nothing was but had been, and all things were that would be, and this I knew for certain holding her, I WAS!

We stay so: me gazing at the burning sea, enchanted; she dreaming or sleeping or nearly so; when quick as flame she leaps up, pointing, "*Ahayani*, look!" I peer in the direction Laurie points, accepting in advance what might appear, fully expecting a vision dreadful, chthonic, preternatural.

"Where?" I call, jumping up to follow her as she rushes off.

"Here, *Ahayani*, over here!"

It was nothing more prepossessing than a gravestone anchored crooked, its two carved figures by the fire's unsteady glare illumined as if set to music, dancing, the wolf and the small girl, dancing on the bare rock by the fire.

Tracing with her fingertip below the bas-relief, Laurie read aloud the brief inscription:

> ALINDA MOON, aged 9
> Beloved daughter of her people
> She was lost and eaten
> by wolves on Grave Island
> April, 1923
> "And a little child shall lead them"

She looked at me, serene but quizzical. "What does that mean?" she asked. "Does it mean she leads them in the dance?"

"That's right," I said, "wolves, and all God's creatures, she leads them in the Peaceable Kingdom in the dance."

"Oh." Then: "Can we see them? Is that place near here, *Ahayani?*"

"It is," I affirmed for the first time in ten years. "It's very near."

EPILOGUE

Lydia
Janet
Letty
Kaleb

Lydia

We all have our obsessions. I guess that's what Jesus meant when he said man didn't live by bread alone. But when Sharp starts turning-on to children, opening his house to them (there must have been two dozen, all around the same age, and all girls); adopting Sim-Sim's family of seven girls while Sim-Sim's off in prison; and, most startling of all, letting Mary Ann stay there while he takes off downtown—well, it struck me as incredible, to say the least. Especially for someone who for years avoided all contact, even clinical, with women! Whose sole companions until I came along had been young boys (one or two were always staying with him, and the whole gang dropped in on him each night), until Marge and Barbara and I started drawing the young boys onto us, and made the parlor of the residence a lounge. Of course that didn't work out either and since Danny's funeral I know Sharp, though he never said a word, blamed *me* for having buggered-up *his* boys. Well, whether or not it's true what they say about him, I figure he was just a little jealous, if not queer. Anyway. . . .

It didn't make sense, this "new Sharp" as the nurses' aids dubbed him, any more than did the old Sharp. Unless, as I said to Marge one day at coffee-break: "He's still scared silly of women and now, robbed of his young men, he's turning-on to little girls."

"What's next?" she said. "The dogs?"

"He's been alone too long," I said, "and getting desperate."

We, the Wilderness

So I wasn't surprised, and neither were the rest of us who knew him, when the morning after the funeral Sharp never showed for work and Emma when she went to clean his office found the note.

"There's a note on Doctor's desk," she said at coffee-break, "an' it's addressed to you." It wasn't sealed and, if I know Emma, probably she'd read it but it made no sense to her. The addressee wasn't, as he usually put, "Matron," nor even the impersonal "Miss Archer" he calls me. It read—was this the "new Sharp" speaking?—"Lydia." I opened it by the window in his office and in late morning sunlight read quickly at first and then more slowly the long page which, at first sight, appeared to be a sort of poem:

> As though you'd never visited an Indian village
> in your life, as though you'd never held my hand, we
> walk along the boardwalk patting children, watched
> from behind racks of drying seaweed by women on
> porches crocheting prayers. Late afternoon. The men
> are all out fishing, thus the prayers, and thus our
> unimpeded passage; were they home we should be
> asked inside for supper, tea at least. You smile, but
> know me well enough we needn't speak. Between us,
> and here-now around us, an awareness of the ends
> implicit in beginnings; lack of impulse; peace. We pass
> and, passing, we remain. I am so glad you share
> this awareness.
>
> The boardwalk ends. Shall we take the bridge
> back, or the path? The path leads into woods which
> are not peaceful if you are not, woods which form an
> ancient ring around our village, themselves bounded
> by older water, evening.
>
> The fear of darkness beneath trees, the ancient

and ancestral fear of penetration. Absence of God.
Perhaps wrath will be loosed upon the world from
this wee box: primeval, past. It is not with us as it
once was, our fear is dense, within; it is not with us,
but within. The worst over, now water and the fire
await us, blood and water.

The earth is fairer now a millionfold nurtured
by the blood of martyrs, for as the mass so martyrs
multiply; the earth is heavier a billionfold bathed in
the blood of maidens, peacemakers whose present of
themselves commences war. We can go back to the
village now and watch the children; we can go back
now to fish and dry seaweed on racks and crochet
prayers, now we can pray; and curse the day we
said Peace, Peace, when there is none.

That was all there was; there was no more . . . no signature,
no salutation—worst, no explanation. I felt nearly as perplexed as
Emma must have. Standing at the window in Sharp's office,
gazing out—the eye is drawn to the straits first, then Grave
Island—pondering the note, an odd thought crossed my mind: I
wondered vaguely whether I was gazing at Grave Island or the
village? Staring idly out the window at the straits between, the
white-caps dancing in sunlight, I had the vague, dreamy impression
I was standing on Grave Island gazing out from one of the
grave-houses at the village, seeing there the hospital, the window
where I stood, and me standing there just out of reach of sunlight,
behind glass: standing, staring, and for a fraction of a
second uncertain where I stood or what I saw!

Then Emma came in: "Janet Elkin's all upset," she said.

Janet rushed into the room, flushed and hyper: "Where's
Doctor?" she demanded. "Kaleb's got the boat ready to go!"

"Go where?" I said, and took my time saying it, because

they always do that, as though *you should know*, and *this is urgent*. "Where is it you want Doctor Sharp to go?"

"Why, Grave Island!" she huffed, and appealed to Emma with an "Is-this-young-girl-impudent-or-ignorant-or-what?" look in her eyes.

"It's old Phereba's little girl," Emma put in quickly, "they think maybe she's over there, across."

Janet

You should have seen that nurse redden like something dreadful struck her and march straight out the door and down the boardwalk clickety-click just like a soldier moves with one thing on his mind, and that thing ugly, like a bullet shot out of a soldier's gun and never stop to say "thank you" or "pardon me" or "kiss my foot." I looked at Emma with a "Well, I never!" look, and Emma ran and shut the door and handed me this letter. I started reading the long part when she turned it over for me to the back where someone'd scribbled, "All my life I've been afraid to be alone, and never known I'd been alone all my life."

I looked at her and started to say "Jesse" because it was the same message they found when they found Jesse Blackstock's boat, but Emma tapped the note and said "Doctor" and pointed. Across. Then I knew what was what and why that nurse flushed and took off, I knew but it was too late to help Dean and, maybe, Laurie.

I grabbed the letter and ran out and down the boardwalk: Sady, you left me a trail of blood, a never-ending. . . . If this is what it comes to, and all because of *him*—father who faked dying, brother who faked father, husband who faked nothing but loved you—I pray beloved daughter, sister, wife, you rest in peace! And I see Josh coming up the wharfwalk, he's running —well, walking briskly, having to step round and over sleeping dogs and Crow—Josh's waving me to "Hurry! They're ready!" This is it. If one more time, Sady, one more time I have go across to Grave Island on your account, you'll never rest! I'll dun you in the next world like you've done me in this one. A bloody sister you have been to me!

The only thing I couldn't figure out was why the sun was shining, shining like it never shone before, when nothing's changed. I hurry down the wharfwalk skirting Crow passed-out and lying with the dogs as usual, but something's in the air and it must be something dying, drowned, or dead if Letty smelled it; because just as I reach the bridge she climbs up on the boardwalk and comes running up behind me: "Lady, Lady, it's that little girl I'm hearin', you know the one they say was eat? She's callin' me."

I stopped full and surprised her so she hadn't any comeback: "Letty," I said, "we were waiting for you. What would a trip across be without you?"

Letty

Honest, I real did hear this child's great-granny, you know her ghost-granny? sayin' she's happy to have back the little child an' singin' *Jesus Loves Me;* sayin' she's happy, more happy with her granny now; she says she's just happy to keep her great-granddaughter with her. Then when we start comin' across they tell me sing along with them, "Letty, you sing along too,"— David Harper says that. But all the while I'm hearin' this young girl-child an' her granny. I don't pretend. See, even those other people, like an old lady that died, you know Mercy Starr's mother? When they finished buryin' her an' start comin' across, I really did see that nice road, the angels on the left an' the right side. An' people were followin' that old lady up to heaven. Then they tell me sing along with 'em, you know *God Be With You?* Then when they finished singin' this old lady started singin' by herself, that hymnin' of hers, *Sweet Bye an' Bye.* Even with Simpson Woodfall's wife I heard it like that. But her favorite hymnin's name was *Onward Christian Soldiers.*

The reason why I knowed it was that little lost girl, you know the one they say was eat?, I's fast asleep in my old house —snow on the ground, 'round December. Then when I lay down a spark must have blowed out, maybe it went under the floorboard 'cause, honest, when I went to bed my house caught fire. I's fast asleep an' woke up really hearin' a small voice, "*Let-*ty, *Let-*ty, wake up, wake up, your house is on fi-er, fi-er" —sayin' that to me. Aiie! jump up out of bed, must be half-asleep; wake up more an' here's just burnin' all 'round. Try feel

167

'round for my Bible an' my shoes, couldn't find 'em, must just grabbed my Indian-song paper an' run out cryin' "Fi-er! Fi-er!" Whit Matson was the first one heard. Then on the third day the cops came, third day after she was lost, cops came: "Letitia, Letitia, your house burnt down, your house burnt down, how did it get on fi-er?" "Oh anyways my old devil-mother forced me keep my stove on, she didn't believe Jesus told me not to worry about wood or anything, she forced me leave my stove on overnight"—I said that to them. An' I told them I think it was that little angel-child, her or her ghost-granny, woke me up.

Geee, after that they ne-ever bother me, say they believe in ghosts now, too.

Anyways when that ol' Janet says they're waitin' on me, an' Kaleb an' his brother an' that nurse an' them is there, I knowed then it was that little lost girl, you know the one they say was eat? I knowed it was her callin' "*Let*-ty, *Let*-ty, come across"—sayin' that, an' that she'd got loose from the funny man we see sometimes. An' the honest reason why I know, see, when I went to dump—goin' on to nighttime when I was still, honest, livin' in my old house—an' I went to dump, you know, my chamberpot? an' it goin' on to nighttime an' near dark? Tide was way down too, an' a lady an' I went down the same time dumpin', but she's far from me; an' we see a guy go walkin' down't the beach an' go awaay *under*-water: shirt, jacket's black, an' his pants was black, just the chest part kind-of white, his hat was orange. He didn't have any rubber-clothes. An' walked waay *under*-water. He didn't have those things for breathin' out. An' this lady an' me both got scared an' run up to our place, an' that same night my old house caught on fire. He never come back up. Was told he must've turned into an otter or somethin', but you know I seen that funny man again on Grave Island an' he was with that little girl makin' her dance! Dancin' round an' dancin' round like they've done these ten years since my house burned an' he caught her warnin' me! I never told nobody, just covered up my eyes. An' that Christian doctor must've saved her from that funny man 'cause, honest, I real heard that little girl sayin' she's happy, more happy with her granny than before; an' she says she's just happy to keep her great-granddaughter with her. I honest really heard 'em in that wind. An' I do hope that funny man, you know when the flood comes? an' the ones that don't believe in Jesus go down to the fire, the *big* fi-er? I do hope that funny man goes where the giants with the really big footprinces went, like that old Chief who tossed his Mrs. overboard.

Kaleb

Dusk on the water, coming back from Grave Island. The straits and passage are the same. The ports the same. Ahead no different from behind: both dark (a few village lights burn feebly; cold stars above Grave Island), both asleep. After the burial, the long wait for the burial, the long death, dusk as usual and everywhere, grey dusk. Everybody's tired from waiting, and everything's the same as before; after, but the same. I dream, no, not of Sady, not Dean even—though his face is still before me, wide-eyed—but of monsters surfacing at dusk just out of sight and when I wake to see who are they? and how ancient? from what depth? they sink below the level of the dusk- and rain-grey water, as though they and all our legends were a dream. Are *we* then, too? Is the same born of the same or of another? If the same, then passage back and forth across the straits between the ports is neither here nor there, we merely pass. If another, then whatever monsters surface from the deep to rock our passage, however much we come and go or wake or sleep in passing, we remain.

Whichever, whether we wake or sleep or dream we are the same and nothing changes; whether we turn to stay or pass on, we remain: Letty sitting aft hymning back toward Grave Island, Sharp amidships and to windward with the night breeze in his face, Josh forward with the tie-rope in his hand, ready to make fast and back to his accounts, Laurie with her granny and the others in the cabin and me topside at the helm, homing this time as a thousand times before—home from the fish-weighing station, home from seaweed picking, home from herringspawing, abalone hunting, clam-digging, jigging, home from burying my sister on Grave Island, home from burying my wife, my son: home to the same berth in the same dock, the same house in the same village, yet not the same and never truly home, but only passing . . . passing the familiar shadowshore between the village and Grave Island, back again, like lights across wide water being stretched and extinguished, we pass and, passing, we remain. . . .

My boat goes on and I go with it. And here forever I remain, a part of the wilderness apart. The world passes us by, but we, the wilderness, endure. And though we never break the surface of the deep, like stars in the night sea we never drown.